The Clarion Call, Vol. 5

An Agorist Writers Workshop Anthology

Edited by:
Genesis Mickel

With stories by:
R.R. Rosalez
Freya Wilde
Roy Baird
Kaeding Sindelar
M. Allyson Szabo
Shashi Kadapa
Lela Markham
Joseph W. Knowles
Billie Holladay Skelley
N.B. Williams
Blake Jessop
Sage Wolkenfeld
Mark Johnson

The Clarion Call, Vol. 5: Fire and Faith
The Agorist Writers Workshop

Cover design by Genesis Mickel
and Eranda Ekanayake

Back cover copy by Justin Fowler

This volume is an official release and copy of
The Clarion Call, Volume 5: Fire and Faith
by the Agorist Writers Workshop, LLC

All proceeds from the original sale of this volume go to support the Agorist
Writers Workshop and the contributing authors.

Published by Agorist Writers Workshop, LLC in the United States of America

www.agoristwritersworkshop.com

WHEN WE LOSE OUR SPIRITUAL VOCABULARY,
WE LOSE MUCH MORE THAN WORDS.
WE LOSE THE POWER OF SPEAKING GRACE,
FORGIVENESS, LOVE, AND JUSTICE
OVER OTHERS.

- JONATHAN MERRITT

CONTENTS

Foreword

I feel honored and blessed to be invited to write the forward for this great volume showing faith and liberty values walking hand in hand. Welcome to Fire & Faith, an anthology featuring the interaction of libertarian principles and spiritual faith. This forward changed as world events evolved during the writing of it.

It's now June of the year 2020. We sure live in interesting times, don't we? Both individual liberty and faith are challenged by world events, so it is fitting that we turned our attention toward that interaction.

Fire & Faith presented a twofold challenge for its contributors... write a story about religious and spiritual faith that also incorporated libertarian principles. Libertarianism and faith sometimes seem incompatible. Libertarianism means maximizing political freedom and autonomy, through choice, voluntary association, personal accountability, and exercise of individual judgment. Some feel faith negates individual liberty because faith requires obedience to a deity or at least a set of tenets, while others live in the tension between obedience to God and freedom from compulsion to obey the secular man. Still others sing in the balance found in the soft overlap of the two. With such a wide mandate, our writers represent a broad scope of interpretations of the theme. How we bring faith and liberty together is an individual interaction that exists in tension, and often, in harmony.

How libertarian of us!

When I wrote "Redemption, Reformatted", I didn't foresee Covid-19 or the homicide of George Floyd at the knee of police. Like most libertarians, I've been accused of being a conspiracy theorist for noting the hardly unnoticeable trend toward tyranny in western societies. Collectivism has been on the rise for decades, but most people insist that you can't complain you're living under authoritarianism if you can buy a café mocha whenever you want.

I chose to focus on an individual test of faith and how God encouraged my main character to meet an obligation he had put upon himself as an atoning consequence of violating the non-aggression principle. Still a redemption story within an individual liberty/voluntaryist framework, but if I'd known what was coming when I wrote it, it would have been a much darker story. I think many of my fellow authors could resonate that sentiment.

During the publication process, we've been provided front row seats to tyranny on parade these past few months, in order to save us from ourselves. A government-ordered stalled economy. Voluntary association suspended. Widespread destruction of small businesses. A higher percentage of unemployed than during the height of the Great Depression. Pervasive social disruption. Suspension of civil liberties. Power centralized. People huddling in their homes "for our own good." Our houses of faith closed because the CDC listed them as more dangerous to reopen than liquor stores and massage parlors. After three months of Coronavirus pandemic shut-down, a cagey public became a powder keg that exploded on the worldwide stage. As I write this, a dozen American cities burn after we watched an authoritarian bully strangle a human being to death and nobody tried to stop him. Cities burn and protesters are clashing on the lawn of the White House. Set up to divide and pit us against each other, it appears democratic collectivism is tearing itself apart.

Show of hands – how many libertarians feel like saying "I told you so"?

When I started writing this forward, my statist friends insisted Covid-19 authoritarian rules were temporary and necessary for our safety. We really don't need buildings to worship in or a faith community that we can interact with face-to-face. If we believe in individual liberty, if we truly have faith, why do we need to worship corporately?

Because we can. Because we want to. Because some of our faith traditions require it. Because faith will be tested and when you're at your most exhausted, it helps to have friends who understand where you're coming from. Because when you're at your angriest, you may need people who can put their arms around you and say, "I get it, but there's a better way." Because, speaking strictly from my own faith tradition, faith demands I overcome fear.

God tests my faith on a daily basis, most especially in times of societal upheaval. He challenges me to act in ways counter to my human inclinations and step out in faith when I am at my most fearful. You'll find several faith traditions represented in this anthology. Speaking from my own, the Christian disciples at Pentecost didn't stay huddled in fear in the upper room. They chose not to be afraid of the statists of their day, but to go out boldly into the streets and preach the gospel. Eventually, the Roman tyrants arrested Christians for assembling against lawful orders. When Peter wrote his second letter about thirty years after Pentecost, the Roman authorities used Christians as human torches to light the cities. You bet they were afraid, but Christian churches exist today because they continued to overcome their fear with faith.

We're not quite so persecuted yet. But angry people who congregate in the streets to throw Molotov cocktails and take their rage out on anyone available based on superficial features, while demanding your vocal consensus - they might test your faith. Fear of a virus you can't see, but "experts" tell you is going to "kill millions" might make huddling in your home feel like a virtuous, good idea (and for some, it might be). But notice, if you are protesting, the experts tell you there is little risk. Which is it? It can't be both, and that contradiction should make us wonder.

Thanks to Covid-19, March 2020 started a watershed event in the world that will affect all of us for the foreseeable future. The strangulation of George Floyd is a continuation of that. It's not an outlier. The authoritarian collectivism that locked us in our homes is the same authoritarian impulse that put a knee on Floyd's throat. There's a metaphorical knee on everyone's throats. Society may now be waking up to that reality.

How do you overcome such fear and darkness?

They say you fight fire with fire, and faith is fire. It's the substance of things hoped for, the essence of things unseen. It's the bright light of hope against an increasingly dark societal situation. Faith doesn't make bad things not happen. It empowers us to live through them. Faith won't stop the madness. It simply helps those who possess it to make sense of the madness. Faith doesn't transform the world by itself, but it provides us the hope and light we need to transform ourselves. Faith gives individual believers the internal check reminding us that we must focus on ourselves rather than meddle in our neighbors' business and call on authorities to enforce conformity.

Faith provides hope that on the other side of darkness and tumult lies a place where the voluntary association and individual liberty we all dream of will be the norm. Maybe collectivism is finally tearing itself apart, and in the wreckage it leaves behind, a new dignity of the individual will rise.

Faith lights a candle in the darkness and transforms our view of the world. It's easy to feel overcome by the darkness around us. Fix your eyes on the fire and let faith carry you through the valley of shadows.

Lela Markham
June 2020

Acknowledgements

Ooooff! We made it to print! This year was one growing pain after another, having formerly had all our publication needs met with former partner Jon Garett of Very Good Books. After he decided to take on new adventures while focusing on his own projects, we were left to find our feet. We almost didn't. It was too much. I almost called it quits. But the support from friends went like this: NO! You can't! There were some tears and maybe even a cell phone thrown across the room. Duly inspired, I persevered.

And, here we are, at last. I decided to forego an Editor's Note this year. I feel I don't have my "public" voice yet. This struggle was causing a further delay, and I am rescued by this decision. There is so much to say about religious freedom in this year, from the shaming or even forbiddance of religious practice to the creation of secular iconography as a replacement for spiritual connection. And ironically, your editor, responsible for helping other people with their words, couldn't find words of her own. The events of the first half of this year make it impossible (for me) to have an unsullied exploration of that place where liberty meets faith, and yet, a gritty and real exploration of religious liberty (dare I say, spiritual awakening) is exactly what is needed right now. Maybe next year in hindsight, these things will be lighter and easier to reflect upon.

So, I will simply leave this with gratitude that we're finally here, and to say a few deep-felt words of thanks to everyone who helped make Fire and Faith happen.

There is a little voluntary team that makes up Agorist Writer's Workshop, and they are my inspiration and my accountability. Without them, this entire project would have withered long before now. Of our many judges past and present, Trent Sehnert, you've been participating from day one, and we look forward to many more years with you on board. Justin Fowler, Annette and

Tyrone Babione, and Mark Johnson, welcome aboard the AWW team! Bokerah Brumley, you held my hand while I transitioned AWW into its own independent publishing house and business entity. Thank you Cara Schulz for generously sharing your connections and advice, and pushing me to not give up. Heather Biedermann, thank you for interviewing AWW in your very first ever Liberty Librarian podcast and for being our ever-enthusiastic cheerleader! Calvin Mickel, thank you for diligently hosting our domain year after year. Richard Walsh, thank you for staying on with us with your important job of submissions scrubber! Thank you Lela Markham for your thought-provoking Foreword on the disturbing juxtaposition between religious liberty and current events in 2020.

Fire and Faith story contributors, I am humbled by the graciousness of each and every one of you. I faced delay after delay, starting from the formidable task of editing and publishing this volume on my own (as a first-timer), to accomplishing everything with a laptop on the fritz, all the way through Covid-19 lock-down and the ways that threw me for a loop. I thought I was surely disappointing you, yet you thanked ME for what I'd been trying to accomplish here. Let me thank you back from the bottom of my heart, truly.

Jon Garett, full-circle back to you, thank you for your original sparkle of an idea in 2014 that led to this project that led to you giving years of your volunteer time to see Clarion Call volumes 1 through 4 through to publication! I have struggled to fill your shoes, but I'm getting there!

Folks, I hope you enjoy these stories crossing so many faiths and time periods, each with a message grounded in liberty. These authors poured their hearts into their work. Thank you so much for your support.

Genesis Mickel
June 2020

A SIMPLE THOUGHT
BY
R. R. ROSALEZ

Rosie knew ever since he was a child that he was different. He knew it in the way that he thought and felt inside. Where others plainly accepted what they were told, Rosie simply could not. Although he would outwardly obey, he could not stop pondering on what seemed to him perfectly normal questions.

He questioned everything really, though he never did so aloud since that was forbidden. Lots of things were outlawed since long before he was born. Any act or behavior that might have at one time been considered morally praiseworthy or what had once been known as "good" had been forbidden for the last 100 years. It was laid out in what Rosie knew and recited daily as The Codex.

The Codex:
It is bad to do good.
Doing good implies that others are bad.
Implying others are bad is wrong and hateful.
Everyone can do as they please so long as it is not good.
I will not do good, in effort, in school, in work, or towards others.
Anyone who does good is evil.

Every morning at sunrise and every evening at dusk, the entire complex would gather and recite The Codex. There was only one rule on the complex—obey The Codex. In all of Rosie's life no one had ever questioned or doubted anything in The Codex. There were other unspoken rules that eventually flowed out of The Codex. Where those rules came from never made sense to Rosie.

One rule was that women could not be named anything that could be called exclusively feminine. All names had to be gender-neutral for females, but specifically feminine for any males. This is why Rosie was named Rosie, and his father was named Kendra, Rosie's mother was named Stacy, and his sister was named Alex.

It was because of The Codex that Kendra ignored Rosie perpetually. Kendra and Stacy were never married, and did not even live in the same cell. Cohabitation with anyone with whom you have had physical relations was expressly forbidden by The Codex. Sexuality and sexual expression were completely boundless. Children were often unable to rightly determine their biological father because many, if not most or all, did not practice monogamy. Organized religion, as it was previously known, had been eradicated by The Codex. Since most religions viewed their beliefs as inherently good, or at the very least better than others, this could not stand in light of The Codex.

It was this concept of organized religion that often captivated Rosie. He would daydream about it regularly and as daydreaming was deemed a nuisance behavior, Rosie spent much of his time doing so. Perhaps the question that puzzled Rosie the most about organized religions was how they developed. Not that he could not comprehend why they developed, but his chief concern was why there was more than one. Organized religion. Organized by whom? For what?

"Rosie!" Stacy called out from behind the wall in their cell.

"Yes, mother." Rosie replied, coming around the wall.

"I know you have a football game today, but I will not be there. I have something else I want to do," Stacy said, while not looking up from her digiphone.

Stacy often ignored Rosie in favor of her digiphone screen. In fact, she abandoned her thoughts to it so completely that she did not notice that her son was neatly dressed and clean.

"I hope you do terribly today in the game. Remember to do your worst and don't display any level of talent. Think of the others."

"Well, I'll just do something or I won't, now won't I?" Rosie shot back, with a small amount of disdain in his tone.

"That's adequately wretched, son. Go on, now, the game started 20 minutes ago."

"I'll go as I please," came the short reply.

Rosie did leave though, and as he left his cell he did so looking rather handsome and fresh. He was sure to be noticed for his good appearance, but not in a good way, or bad really.

Three abrupt knocks sounded at the door of Stacy's cell. She came quickly to answer it but found the door had already been opened. In the doorway stood four unkempt and surly looking men.

After a few seconds of staring blankly at Stacy and each other, the four men parted allowing a small woman to enter. Her name was Charley, and she was awful at her job. Her hair was messy, she wore what looked like pajamas, and was most unhelpful in her visit. Nevertheless, it was communicated to Stacy that her son had been arrested for doing good and was therefore guilty of a hate crime.

"How could this be?" Stacy thought. She made sure that he left well after the game had started, or at least when it was supposed to start. What could have been the problem?

When she arrived at the Grand Council hall, she saw very plainly what the problem had been. Standing there in chains was her son, Rosie. He was standing tall, with clean, neatly parted hair wearing a pristinely-kept suit and tie. He was almost breathtaking to look at in stark contrast with the careless and disheveled look of everyone else.

Stacy looked at her son for only a moment and then quickly at the ground. She could feel something like a lump growing in her throat and after a very uncomfortable, albeit quick moment, gulped as quietly as she could manage. She didn't understand why, but she suddenly felt very odd. She didn't like it, but she could not evade it, even though she knew she was unclean and a visible mess, she certainly felt more so upon seeing her son.

The council showed up late by at least half an hour, and when they did they wasted no time in moving to judgment.

"It's evident that there is no need for a trial here; we can all see that the accused is guilty," they mumbled amongst themselves.

Finally, one of the council members stood up.

"Let's get this over with then," said the standing council member. "Rosie, you are charged with being good and therefore committing an act of evil as defined by The Codex. Did you knowingly dress and comb your hair in such a way as to appear better than others?"

"I dressed myself and brushed my hair because not doing it didn't make sense anymore," replied Rosie.

"Rosie, do you understand what The Codex is?" asked the council member.

"Well, yes," started Rosie, "but, doesn't my understanding violate The Codex? Doesn't your asking me if I understand threaten to make me feel bad for possibly not understanding?"

At this remark another council member stood up and began shouting.

"You DARE talk back to the council?? To question The Codex?!"

"Who am I to not?" asked Rosie calmly. "Again, if the rule is to be not good then the right thing to do is to question The Codex. Why is it good to obey The Codex, but not evil because it is good? It just doesn't make sense to me anymore. It is nothing more than tyranny disguised as virtue."

"Well," began the second council member, "it appears we have

4

ourselves a troublemaker. Since the accused has not acknowledged nor submitted himself to The Codex, we must now add another charge to his case, blasphemy. The penalty for such a crime is nothing less than death."

The entire council including Stacy let out an audible gasp. Rosie seemed completely unfazed by the development and instead began to speak further about The Codex.

"You can kill me if you want. In fact, you will have to kill me, because I cannot and will not stop speaking out about the incoherence of The Codex. It is an exercise in willful ignorance. You say good is bad and bad is good, but if that's the case then who determines when a thing is actually good or bad? It's all just a shifting of the wind isn't it? It's good to obey The Codex, but The Codex itself declares that good is evil. So you cannot escape it.

"I should not have to lower myself so that others do not feel short. I can do nothing about their being short. So I will squat low no more. I should not have to look a mess if I have the means to clean myself and look presentable. I cannot control what others do; if they choose to look and be dirty and unkempt that should be their choice to make, not mine and certainly not yours. That's what this whole thing is about, isn't it? Control. Well, you cannot control me. You do not determine what is truth. Twenty-two hundred years ago a man lived named Jesus, and-"

The entire council shouted at this name and the whole scene turned to chaos.

"Throw him into the pit!!"

"Shut up!! Shut up!! Don't you DARE say that name!!"

"Away with him! He must die!"

More shouts like these spewed forth from the lips of the council members. They were enraged and filled with such hatred, the likes of which Stacy had never seen or imagined possible. Once they had somewhat regained their composure the council told her that Rosie was scheduled to have a death hearing tomorrow at 1pm, immediately followed by the carrying out of his death sentence.

Rosie stood quiet. None of it made sense. Stacy was quickly escorted out of the room and reminded to be on time for the evening recitation of The Codex. As she looked back she saw her son hit over the head and dragged away towards the pit. "What in the world is going on?" Stacy wondered. "Why did this woman's name spark so much rage? No, wait, Rosie said it was a man. A man with a masculine name?? Twenty-two hundred years ago?? None of it made sense." Stacy snapped out of it and rushed off to recite The Codex.

Stacy had been back in her cell for hours but couldn't sleep. After the evening recital of The Codex she just could not shake what she had seen and heard. Who was this Jesus? Why did he have a masculine name? Why did the Council seem to know who he was and respond with such rage?

Stacy went to Rosie's room to see if she could find some answers. When she opened the door she didn't see anything spectacular. Rosie's room was somewhat cleaner than normal but still quite a mess.

She began to look around, something she had never thought to do or even had reason to do previously. She looked around for ten minutes, but what to her seemed like an hour. She threw herself down on his bed in exasperation.

Stacy knocked something off the bed that landed with a heavy thud. It must have been under the pillow. When she looked on the floor she saw what looked like a small rectangular box. She couldn't quite tell what was in it, but it felt heavy. She looked on the cover and saw words she had never seen before. "HOLY BIBLE" beneath it were four letters. "NKJV" None of these made sense to Stacy. As she looked closer she began to realize this was not a box, but a book.

It looked to be at least a hundred years old, if not more. When she opened the cover she saw she was right. The book was published in 2040, over a hundred and fifty years ago. "What was this doing in Rosie's room under his pillow?" Stacy wondered. She noticed a piece of paper hanging out towards the back of the book marking a specific location. When she opened it a wafer thin paper fell out. On it she could just make out some writing.

"Rube, I hope this blesses you and that you come to know the Truth of Jesus Christ our Savior. The Truth will set you free, brother. God is good, always remember that! In Christ, Tad."

Stacy didn't know what to make of it, but she was intrigued by the name that was beginning to become familiar to her. The name of Jesus seemed to be something important not only to this Rube and Tad, but also to her son. Whoever this Jesus is and what this book says had to be what caused Rosie to act so crazy. Maybe she could find something in here that would help to exonerate her son.

She began feverishly reading right where the page had fallen out.

"Let not your heart be troubled; you believe in God, believe also in Me." No, nothing there. She continued down further. "Jesus said to him, "I am the way, the truth, and the life. No one comes to the Father except through Me."

"What does this mean?" Stacy pondered. She continued to read, and in fact went all the way to the beginning of the section called, "The Gospel of John," where she read "In the beginning was the Word and the Word was with God, and the Word was God."

Before she realized it she was finished with this section of the book and near the end she read, "And truly Jesus did many other signs in the presence of His disciples, which are not written in this book; but these are written that you may believe that Jesus is the Christ, the Son of God, and that believing you may have life in His name."

Stacy was startled when her alarm went off for the morning

recital of The Codex. She had just finished reading the section of the book called Isaiah 5 which reads, "Woe to those who call evil good, and good evil; Who put darkness for light, and light for darkness; Who put bitter for sweet, and sweet for bitter!" She was all the more fascinated with what this all meant. She closed the book and ran out the door, thinking on what she had just read.

After the sunrise recitation of The Codex, she rushed back to Rosie's room to continue reading. Lunch time came and went and she never stopped reading. Finally her digiphone alerted her that it was now time for the death hearing of her son.

Stacy rushed out of her cell and towards The Grand Council hall. When she arrived she saw her son being escorted in. He looked peaceful, not at all afraid, and certainly not angry or bitter. It was then that Stacy began to wonder if this peace that he had was because he too had read what was in the Holy Bible book.

Stacy's thoughts were interrupted by the appearance of the council members. If she saw peace in the eyes of her son, what she saw in the eyes and faces of the council was absolute hatred. Their faces were contorted with unabashed revulsion and loathing. They were very quick in their speech this time.

Without much discussion, one of the men stood and said with such malice, "Do you wish to recite The Codex?"

"The Codex is a false religion," said Rosie with heartsease. "I will no longer be under that yoke. It is not truth and therefore not worth having. I have the truth, and the truth has set me free."

"SILENCE!" shouted the man on the council.

"I, Melody, do hereby recommend that you be sentenced to death for the crime of hatred and evil acts against the citizens on the complex and blasphemy of The Codex. Do you have anything else to say for yourself before you're sentencing?"

Rosie was silent.

"Are there any opposed?" shouted Melody.

Again silence from everyone.

"This man has been found guilty and will be put to death at

3pm outside of the complex on the hill of condemnation. Take him away!" cried Melody.

Stacy looked down at her digiphone and saw that it was already almost 2:30. She could not comprehend what was happening. She wanted to be cold and feel nothing, but she was definitely feeling something. Whatever it was she pushed it down and quickly followed what had now developed into a crowd.

It seemed the council let word get around there was going to be an execution. The last execution had been over thirty-five years ago. So naturally, everyone in the complex wanted to come see. In fact, Stacy noticed there were people going door to door at every cell calling people to come witness what happens to those that disobey The Codex.

She looked around again and found her son. He had a busted lip now and some blood on his cheek. Stacy guessed that it was from the council members who clearly had great disdain for him. They walked ahead of Rosie and at a brisk pace, as if they were eager to be rid of him.

It was a long walk, but Rosie stood tall and took long, measured strides. He looked serene, as if he was just going for a walk around the complex and found comfort in it. Stacy almost thought he looked happy.

When they reached the hill of condemnation, the council repeated the sentence and Melody withdrew a pistol from his waistband. Stacy still couldn't emotionally grasp what was going on. In her stomach she began to feel twisted up, almost like she was seeing something bad happen that was genuinely bad.

"Do you have any final words before your condemnation is carried out, you hateful do-gooder?" Melody asked. His face was a ball of disgust mixed with rage.

"Yes," said Rosie. "I do. And this is the condemnation, that the light has come into the world, and men loved darkness rather than light, because their deeds were evil. For everyone who hates the light does not come to the light lest his deeds should be exposed. But he who does the truth comes to the light, that his deeds may be clearly seen, that they have been done in God."

"AAAGGHHHHHHHH!!!!" At the word "God" Melody roared and fired a single shot at Rosie's head. He collapsed on the ground as blood spilled out of his temple.

The crowd let out an audible groan as Rosie's body collapsed into a lifeless heap. Then the whispers began to spread.

"He was always so weird anyways," said one girl. "He always seemed to struggle to not do good."

"What's he mean saying the name of God, everyone knows there is no such thing," said an older lady.

"Yes, he was odd wasn't he?" said another. "That Rosie should have never tried to do good, that's always gonna end bad. What's so hard about not doing good? For shame."

His mother Stacy could see it too. All the other children in the complex got along well enough. They could easily ignore any impulse they may have towards good. Good is evil, after all. It was their mantra, their deeply held convictions that had to be accepted at all costs. This was their religion.

"Religion," Stacy pondered as the crowds began to thin and leave. "Could it be?" she continued in her thinking, "that The Codex really and truly represented a sort of religion in itself?" The cognitive dissonance tore through Stacy's mind and led her to a host of other questions.

"Could it be that The Codex was wrong? Could it be that sentencing her son to death was an actual evil committed by The Codex belief system?" The questions kept flooding her mind.

She looked down again at her son, Rosie. His eyes were open still, looking blankly into nothingness. Why, only ten minutes earlier he stood so strong and looked so sure of himself. He really did look so handsome in his suit and tie. His hair was neatly brushed. The whole scene unwillingly made Stacy think of her son in a new way. Why hadn't she ever seen him like this? He was tall, handsome, and filled with such potential. Her eyes began to well with tears as she pondered on all the missed opportunities of success he could have had.

"Good is evil!!" Stacy shouted at the top of her lungs as she began to sob violently into her hands.

Stacy shook with rage. This would have never happened if she didn't show favor, if she didn't have any good feelings towards her son. She must stop thinking this way, she knew she must. Yet, she could not stop shaking and crying in agony. No matter how hard she fought against it, Stacy could no longer deny an unmistakable reality. She loved her son!

"Good IS EVIL!!!" she screamed again.

The rage she felt, the anger and the heart-shattering pain racked every fiber of her being. She cried until she was hoarse and could barely hold herself up. Eventually she stopped trying. Lying in a heap next to her dead son, a simple yet profound thought entered her mind.

"Good...good is...good is GOOD!" Stacy finally muttered aloud what she had already begun to know when she witnessed Rosie walking so confidently to his death. Everyone else saw a fool. Stacy saw her son: a good son, a strong, brave, and handsome son.

She could no longer deny what was so plainly obvious to her. In that moment her heart turned from pain-stricken anguish to relief, then wonder, and finally to joy! If good is good, then evil is wrong. There is such a thing as truth, and it can be known. The law of such truth is written on the hearts of men and she knew it as clear as the sun was shining.

Many moments later, Stacy finally pulled herself to her feet. Her face was calm and her demeanor strong. Stacy began her long walk back towards the complex. The sun was low on the horizon, and dusk was fast approaching. One thought resounded loudly in her mind. One thought gripped her tightly and held her in a peace that surpasses all understanding.

"Good is good. Truth is good. God IS GOOD."

HOLDER 76
BY
FREYA WILDE

Holder 76 needed to get to the birth before the Watchers did. While balancing his staff horizontally in one fist, he fled. Chuffing as he labored in a careful sprint across slippery thick spongy yellow pads called Gri-floats that made up the only transport between places on the water planet, Upik. The end of his long, brown robe clapped behind him in the wind as if it was his private audience, cheering and urging him on.

Finally, he jogged up the many steps to a main street bridge of a smallish town constructed completely on bridges. With each step he took as he caught his breath, the staff tapped an echo in the narrow alley. The staff would defend him if the Watchers attacked. Its sharp pointy end striking the cement road reassured him.

Holder gazed at the sun in its zenith overhead. Its rays beat down on his face between the layers of bridges arching in all directions above. Some of the suspended footpaths that crisscrossed overhead were simple, slender rope-woven walkways, while other bridges were massive acres wide cityscapes spanning between other bridges piled high in residential areas, houses, and apartments stacked end to end. Some of the footpaths between the neighborhoods had intricate arches that connected together in places, cupping quirky little tea or coffee shops. Even bustling restaurants tucked between them on different sized platforms. He clenched the staff in agitation. He'd have to walk through the busy crowded place and he needed to be quick about it to make it to the birthing of the child foretold to be born this night. Peering down at the water splashing against one of the massive pylons that drove deep under water and supported it all, he took a moment to lament the difficult task he knew was ahead of him.

Quickly passing through the crowded streets, past various shops, taverns, and street vendors selling aromatic fish packets his mouth watered, but he had no time to eat. Holder flew past little fairs and open markets of freshly grown vegetables and fruits raised in pocket gardens and green houses. Passing a little garden behind a row of freshly constructed brick townhouses, Holder stopped to stare at a mother and child. The infant in the young mother's arms was a newborn, its pink cheeks in a scrunched up face, so tiny and perfect. The baby's ariils growing out of the top of its head were pale, transparent slim stocks about the length of the child's tiny webbed fingers. It wouldn't be until onset of puberty that the ariils would change into the color determined by the child's genetics. Holder's own ariils were light green and currently writhing in agitation. Holder's face fell. His hand on his staff trembled. Resolutely he turned away. Quickly he moved on through the city.

He passed by a Quantum Net Temple, where the Watchers worship. Watchers, he thought in annoyance, the bane of Holders. Self-consciously, he pulled his brown Holder's robe tighter about his wiry body and looked down and away as he hurried past the temple's doors engraved with a huge diagram of the quantum Block Sphere. The last thing he needed was more of the fanatical Watchers to stop him from getting to the child before it was born. A hand fell on his shoulder. Holder spun about, staff held in both his hands ready to defend himself. A Quantum Net Temple priest stood before him, dressed in a priest's typical black robe of his religion, barefoot and blindfolded with a black bandana across his eyes and tied tightly behind his head. "My son." Said the priest "Won't you enter the Temple and give yourself to the great creator?"

Holder said nothing. He felt disgusted by the blind man and all he stood for. And he searched the crowd for any of the Temple Watchers, the soldiers for the Quantum religion. But he saw none of the black clad army in the crowd.

Relaxing a little, Holder straightened, "I'm on business, old man. Best be on your way." Holder was about to gently jab the priest away from him when the priest's hand shot out and took hold of the end of the staff, stopping Holder from touching him. Holder's eyes widened. He tried to pull the staff out of the priest's grip. "How...are you able to see me?" He gasped.

"We are all one with the fabric of space, Holder. We are all watchers waiting for connection with the expanding infinity, my son."

"How did you know who I am?" demanded Holder. The priest seemed to be staring right at his face through the black fabric, but Holder knew, everyone knew, Temple priests were blind from birth. It was not possible for the priest to see him, and yet, somehow this priest knew he was from the Order of the Holders. "How did you know I am a Holder?" demanded Holder again.

"There is more than one way to see, Holder. Surrender your mission, come inside the Temple, and see for the first time what our world has lost," said the priest, taking a step closer toward Holder, a beatific smile leering at him. The priest's voice was full of worshipful zeal as he continued to preach at Holder. "Behold, for the first time Holder, connect with everything. Watch with us."

Holder felt sick at the priest's words, "The Holder prophecy cannot be denied! You speak lies and you're wicked!" He screamed, jerking the staff so hard out of the priest's hands, Holder fell back a few steps, but quickly regained his balance.

The staff holder began running through the streets, far away from the temple and its greedy priest. When he finally reached the other end of the town, he peered down off the end of a bridge and saw several Gri-float roads trailing off in different directions across the water so distant he couldn't see where they led. After pointing the staff towards the roads, the tracker program within the staff gave a little tug toward the right. "East it is, then," he said to himself. Hurrying down the stairs to reach the surface of the water and the Gri-float roads, halfway down he gave a sharp cry as he tripped and tumbled down hard cement steps to a small landing. Dazed and on his back, he was surrounded by four Temple Net Watchers balancing on their nimble feet in various stances of battle readiness. Holder thought it must have been one of them who tripped him. Garbed in black loose clothing with black bandanas covering the tops of their heads, their eyes smoldered at him through eye slits; the Watchers were as reedy legged as some migratory water birds. But they also reminded Holder of sharp beaked birds of prey perched above and below him on the stairs and railings. The nearest Watcher jumped towards him, followed by another.

Rolling swiftly to the left and barely avoiding being stomped by the Watcher, Holder whipped out his staff, cutting them down as he sprang to his feet. Holder began to run down the stairs to escape, but the Watchers on the ledge threw himself at him as he ran past, causing both to fall over the ledge and hit the water together. Immediately, a Watcher pushed Holder back under water when he surfaced. Holder was shocked to feel a knife slice at the ariils on the top of his head. The Watcher was trying to drown him by removing his ariils, his way to breathe under water. Holder tried to pry the hands off his head, but failed. Panicking, he felt for his staff, and was relieved when he felt it floating next to his hand and grasped it, stabbing hard at the Watcher with the staff's business end. The Watcher let go and Holder broke through the surface. Floating face down, blood seeped from the side of the Watcher's head where Holder had stabbed him, clouding the water around the still body.

Starting to swim for the nearest Gri-float, Holder only got a few strokes before another Watcher landed as lightly as a dancer on a torn off chunk of Gri-float floating next to him. The Watcher landed a kick to Holder's head, causing it to snap back. The momentum from the kick caused the Watcher to splash down off the chunk and away from Holder. Despite being kicked dizzy, Holder managed to keep swimming for the Gri-float, taking in more water than air it seemed, but he swam as hard as he could. The webbing between Holder's fingers helped him greatly to pull him through the water, the staff tucked into his belt.

Reaching rough, rock-hard rhizomatous roots which threaded the floats together made it easy in his weakened state to pull himself up onto a Gri-float's slippery surface, where he lay panting from exertion. Unfortunately, yet another Watcher landed in the middle of the float and proceeded to beat Holder where he was sprawled.

Still clinging miraculously to his staff, Holder roared in outrage and struck at the Watcher so hard in the legs, his staff broke in half. Whether the Watcher lay unconscious or dead, Holder didn't care. Stabbing him in the heart with one sharp end of his broken staff, Holder made sure the Watcher wouldn't awaken to attack him again. Two of the Watchers were dead. Stunned, he stared at his precious broken Holder staff in disbelief. The tracker was destroyed, and now he had no way to find the child before it was born.

The third Watcher who'd fallen into the water after kicking him had swum faster than Holder had thought. He'd been so engrossed in contemplating what he was going to do now that his staff was broken, he hadn't noticed the Watcher almost upon him. The Watcher pulled himself up on the Gri-float so fast, Holder barely had time to block his face with his arm before being pummeled and kicked the same way the other Watcher had beat him. Holder blocked and tried to kick back but felt his legs getting as heavy as someone whose feet were hardened in cement blocks and tossed into the deep. When the Watcher put his hands round Holder's neck and squeezed, Holder stared at the Watcher's eyes burning with determination to end him.

A startled expression opened the Watcher's eyes wide. Holder had stabbed him in the side with one of the sharp ends of his broken staff. As the light died in the Watcher's eyes, Holder pushed the lifeless body off of him. He stared around warily. There had been four Watchers to begin with; he searched to see where the last one was. Holder saw him, or her, still up on the stairs, gazing down at him and the other dead Watchers. Rather than attacking Holder, the Watcher took off running up the stairs to disappear back into the city.

Stumbling off the Gri-float, Holder got back onto the cement stairs, staggering all the way up, the two halves of his broken staff were in each of his hands. He tossed them into the ocean on the way up. The sun was hours past its zenith. He hurried back into the busy walkways- time was running out if he was going to make it to the birth before sundown. He hoped luck would be with him and there would be no further Watcher attacks.

Stopping after a time to gaze up and all around, Holder desperately sought the telltale neon blue laser light that always shone from the top of a Data Pole. His soaked shoes squelched in discomfort as he strode further into the city. Again and again, with an ominous sense of urgency riding him, he searched above and between the bridges for the blue light of a pole. Then there, he started jogging toward the only blue Data Pole light that he'd seen in this small city. It was a faint blue light that shot at a slant toward the clouds, but it was there. His soaked robe clung to him like seaweed and chafed his skin. But as he jogged toward the blue shaft of light, it made him think of home, Holder Keep. A castle built on a bridge far to the north where all one hundred Holders lived when they weren't on a mission. Feelings of warmth at the thought of home pushed back the cold in his bones. He imagined that right then the other Holders were probably finishing their midday meal, a roaring fire of dried out old Gri-float wood would be crackling in the hall's big hearth, warming them all despite outside's icy and stormy north sea crashing against the impenetrable Holder Keep.

When he arrived, it was only to discover the Data Pole gripped between two ancient, giant Gri-float roots. The yellow-green roots had grown over and around the square sides of the pole and partially over the top, which resulted in its light being not only fainter than it would've been, but the Data Pole slanted to the side causing its blue light to shine at an off angle instead of shooting straight up as it was supposed to. No wonder he'd had a hard time spotting the pole.

Holder shook his head at its neglect. There were only a hundred Holders total on Upik. Out of those hundred, only First Holders, sainted Holder numbers 1-10, are allowed unlimited access to the Data Poles. And there were a limited amount of Data Poles on the water planet. Holder 76 had only ever had access to a Data Pole five brief times in his life. It filled him with longing to remember it. He swallowed the yearning in shame, and forced himself to remember his duty. Holders 1-10's objectives were for them to know, not him. He knew this. He felt the cold return. Shivering, he thought of the child that he must find before it is born, his sole purpose as a Holder.

Clenching his fists determinedly, he spoke into the round screened hole on the front of the pole. "Holder 76, asking for access."

There was no response.

"Emergency!" He cried, feeling panicky. How would he find the child without a staff? "This is Holder 76, asking for Data access. My staff broke in a fight against four Watchers. Tell me how to find where the birth will be, please."

Silence.

"Please..." Holder begged it, resting his forehead against the pole.

The blue light blinked out once. A neutral voice spoke from the pole, "Retrieve Holder 32's staff from above the bar at the tavern called the Fisherman's Ease. Make haste."

"Thank you for finally answering," Holder's voice raised slightly, "But, that's it?" After waiting a while longer to see if whoever had answered would say more, Holder added as he wrapped his arms round his shivering wet body, "Well, I'll do my best to uphold the prophecy's decree." Holder's head hung. He said softly, "I'm Holder 76."

There was no further communication from the pole, and Holder tiredly moved away from it with heavy legs. He felt like a half drowned bridge-rat. Forcing himself to trudge back through the streets, up many more stairs, further to the higher bridge-ways where he knew the neighborhoods with taverns would be, it took an hour of miserable walking to find the Fisherman's Ease. The place was in a shady looking side path that smelled of garbage and fish waste. Standing in front of the door of the tavern, he was furious at his situation and angry at whomever it was who'd spoken to him from the Data Pole. The person's cavalier attitude toward his plight to fulfill his duty and get to the birth in time was too much to bear in his physical exhaustion and anxiety to finish his duty.

Banging through the doors, he wiped his long, limp ariils off his face and went right to the long water-wood bar constructed of old hard Gri-float roots.

The place smelled of spilt beer, sweat, and hard liquor fumes, but it was warm, and for just a moment he let the warmth of the place soothe his sore muscles. Leaning against the polished dark bar, Holder looked up at the dusty ancient Holder staff mounted against the dark wall behind the bar. A brass plaque underneath the staff said, The staff of Holder 32.

Holder frowned up at the mounted staff as he downed a shot of hard liquor someone had left at the bar. The sordid story of Holder 32. He'd heard the story of Holder 32, who had left the Order after having been instructed to complete a mission much like he was currently on. Holder 32 had sold his precious staff to buy liquor, which resulted in the other 99 Holders to ostracize him. After only a few years, drinking killed Holder 32. Holder 76 imagined it must have been this place where he frequented; perhaps 32 had even died right here in this tavern, and that's how the place had gotten his staff.

Hundreds of bottles of different colored alcohol were lined up against the wall on the shelf below the staff.

A barman with a spontaneous bone-white toothed grin asked, "Can I getcha anythin'?"

Shaking his head once, Holder ordered, "Bring down the staff." He pointed at the staff with his chin. "I'm taking it."

The young barman peered up at the staff. "I can't. It's not mine. It belongs to the tavern's owner."

"Is the owner in?"

Shaking his head at Holder as if Holder was crazy, the barman laughed, "No." The barman then looked the other way to tend to another customer, writing Holder off by showing him his back.

"Do you even know what that is?" Holder shouted at the barman's back. The young man didn't even turn his head to acknowledge Holder had spoken. Holder snorted, thinking them so ignorant they didn't even know how precious the thing was that was mounted on the wall over the bar.

Knowing what he had to do, Holder marched down the length of the bar, went behind it, strode up underneath the staff, and plucked it off the wall.

"Hey," the barman said when he noticed what Holder had done, "Hey, you can't do that!"

"I already have." Holder started to stalk away with Holder 32's staff. His long brown robe, which had mostly dried out, flew out behind him as he strode at a fast pace across the tavern. Pressing the tracker button on its side, Holder immediately felt the gentle tug pulling the staff toward the east. Holder smiled. He'd find the child yet before it was born.

But there in the front doorway stood the fourth Watcher who'd run away from him earlier. He was with two more new Watchers, all of them garbed in the typical Watcher black clad loose clothing and black bandanas over their eyes.

As Holder fled toward the back exit, he knocked down the barman as he dashed by.

"Hey! You can't do that!" The barman yelled again in indignation.

The three Watchers took pursuit. One of them dumped

patrons' drinks as he pursued, resulting in shouts of outrage. Holder could almost feel the Temple worshipper's zealous breath on his neck.

Bursting through the backdoor, Holder was dismayed to find himself not on a walkway leading away from the bar, but instead on a tiny balcony that overlooked white caps on the water far below. Every way he turned, he saw there was nowhere to go. The little space was too far away from any other bridge for him to jump to. He'd have to toss himself into the ocean if he wanted to get away.

He jumped. Holding the staff in both hands, he tucked it vertically next to his body. Feet first, while fervently delivering the Holder Prophecy to himself all the long way down. "The child must be found before its birth . . ."

His spine jolted with electricity when he hit the water and he buckled with pain. Taking gasping breaths after he'd surfaced, he noticed Holder 32's staff bobbing up and down in the water next to him. He grabbed it.

Gazing briefly up at the tiny balcony he'd jumped from, he saw the three Watchers looking down at him. Holder gambled that the Watchers weren't as crazy as he. He guessed right, they did not jump in after him. The sun was hours past its zenith. Holder swam as fast as he could make his battered body go, and was soon out of the Watcher's sight under a low bridge.

Coming across a small untethered Gri-float pad, Holder climbed upon it and rested for a minute. "I need to get to the birth!" He shouted in frustration, pounding one fist against the Gri-float. Peering round, he brightened when he saw an unattended airboat tied up to someone's private dock. It was idling quietly.

⌘

Hours later, with the stolen airboat, Holder 76 pulled up next to a tiny village built entirely on Gri-float pads with no bridges in sight. After all these years, Holder 32's staff still worked well and had guided him there. With a half-smile, he silently thanked the sad, infamous dead Holder. "You may not have failed after all, 32." As his gaze quickly took in the village, he decided he didn't want to know what it might be like in this place during the rainy season. The little huts were hand-built of hard, tough reeds, and the walls were dried, oily, thick seaweeds. The huts bobbed on the floats with every little ripple and swell of the ocean. The salty air smelled of sun dried fish, soap, and wet rope.

After tying the airboat to a dock anchor, he started marching past huts, the staff tugging him forward. The Gri-floats were linked together by their humongous rhizomatous roots, which Holder walked or leapt over. The sun was just starting to set on the horizon, so he quickened his pace. "Hurry!" He told himself while searching the tiny village of huts.

Shortly, Holder heard a woman moaning and knew he'd arrived just in time to the right hut. Pushing open a woven mat of seaweed with the end of the staff, he bent his head down to peer through the doorway.

He saw a very pregnant woman whose pearl-decorated crown of silky green ariils writhed in distress as she strained to give birth. She was so beautiful, Holder's breath caught. Her dark purple almond-shaped eyes and abalone skin covered in a pearlescent sheen of sweat complimented her green contorting ariils. A brown aquatic animal skin was draped partially over her naked body, which gave her a measure of modesty. An elderly woman and another man Holder surmised must be the father of the child were the only ones in attendance for the birth.

"Who are you?" demanded the man when he noticed Holder. His pale blue ariils were stiff with alarm and challenge.

"Holder 76," Holder said. He ducked his head further down and completely entered the hut.

"A Holder?" spat the man, his eye's widening in anger. "What do you want?" he growled, crossing the room in just a couple of steps to stand in front of Holder. The man's right webbed hand rested on a long silver filleting knife hanging from his side.

"I'm here because of the prophecy." Holder placed his own webbed hands one over the other on top of Holder 32's staff, explaining as if the man was a child that needed schooling, "It is foretold that the Prophecy Child will be born this day. This staff," Holder lifted the staff up a bit, "led me here." Holder tried to take a step closer to see the progress of the birth, but the man leaned, blocking Holder's view with his body.

A keening of pain and straining came from the mother. Holder was much taller than the man so that it was nothing for him to cock his head and see the old woman on her knees, down before the mother, assisting with the birth.

"Your baby is almost here, Challa. One more push, and you'll meet your child," encouraged the matron in a soothing tone, both hands guiding the child from the birth canal.

Such a tiny, sweet head, Holder thought with regret. The ariils on the child's head were limp and so pale they were almost translucent.

Suddenly, the child fully slipped into the old woman's hands. "Oh, lovely child," she beamed, smiling up at Challa. Two small, bright beams of light shone out of the cracks of the newborn's half open eyes. "His eyes!" the mother of the child cried in alarm.

"The babe is as was foretold. A new beginning for us all, in all places, for all time." The midwife smiled triumphantly at the baby now cradled in its mother's arms.

The child does look perfect, Holder thought. But regardless, the time had come for him to do what he was sent to do, as the Holder prophecy had foreseen must be done.

Knocking the father protecting the mother and his baby aside easily with the staff, Holder rushed toward the newborn, the staff now automatically powered-up. A blue light shot out one end of it.

A Watcher dove through the window and tackled him to the ground before Holder could do what he believed he must do.

"You don't understand!" Holder cried, fighting to get his staff into position to fulfill his destiny. "The Prophecy Child must die!"

He screamed as he fought.

"What are you talking about, you madman!" cried the man who Holder believed was the child's father, who'd by then gotten to his feet and was standing over Holder warningly with his wicked-looking fillet knife in his hand.

Holder recognized the Watcher as the fourth, the one who'd survived when they first attacked him that morning on the cement steps. It seemed a lifetime ago now. The Watcher squatted on Holder's chest, one of his hands around Holder's throat, ready to crush it, to stop him from killing the newborn.

"It is the duty... of all Holders to be ready... for the birth, and the nearest Holder to... the foretold birth must be the one... to kill the child immediately... after its... birth," Holder recited in short gasps. The Watchers grip around his neck held firm.

"I know of your ridiculous Holder prophecy," sneered the Watcher straddling him.

The Watcher peered out the window. "You're too late," he said with satisfaction. "The sun just slipped below the horizon."

"No," Holder whispered, dread filling him. "I failed." Moaning, he dropped the now useless staff.

A puzzled expression on his face, the father of the child frowned at Holder. "What do you mean, Prophecy Child?"

The old woman gave Holder a smug expression. Staring at her, Holder knew she knew what Holder was talking about, and he was appalled to see that she was glad the Prophecy Child would live.

At that moment, the world was plunged into shadow, and a strong wind blew through the village, tearing and sending the dried seaweed roofing and siding of the huts to lift and blow wildly. Everyone else was ignoring Holder now. The Watcher who'd sat on him left the hut. Through the window, Holder could see in the night sky all the stars shining brighter than he'd ever seen them shine before. The old woman, mother, and newborn stayed in the hut with the father who was standing over the women and baby protectively, his knife still out and his angry gaze never leaving Holder. Just before Holder left to see what was happening outside the hut, he turned to the family and said, "You're safe. It's too late. There's no reason for me to harm your child now."

Outside, the Watcher smiled and started to say, "Your Holders 1-10..." Holder's eyes widened, shocked that the Watcher knew that much about them. The Watcher smirked, "Yes, I know about your secret Holders 1-10. They've lost their control of this world for good." He glanced at the sky, "Rejoice, we're free of your little cult's chains."

From inside the hut, Holder heard Challa, the newborn's mother, cry out as a light so bright shone out of the hut it almost blinded them all. Holder and the Watcher gasped, their arms held up before their faces against the brilliance.

Then the light from the hut coalesced into a single ball and shot directly through the roof of the hut into space where it exploded. Its fiery illumination seemed to blend with every bright star in the night before breaking up into millions of tiny sparks that fell upon Upik, like snow. Two of the tiny star like objects fell down near the hut. The brightness of the spheres flickered out slowly into fist sized balls of soft calm white light.

Holder peered into the shack. The newborn was gone. The child's mother was weeping into the old woman's arms as she cooed softly to the grieving mother.

"This was meant to be," Holder could hear the old woman say. "He was the Prophecy Child."

Holder was afraid. He'd failed the Order of the Holders and didn't know what would become of him with no mission. What was his purpose now? Everything was happening too fast.

Holder saw the Watcher take off his black bandana and walk up to one of the spheres, his dark green ariils writhed excitedly as he closed his eyes. When he opened them, his eyes had a detached, faraway shuttered look. "I'm in the Net. I can see . . . everything," the Watcher exclaimed.

"What do you mean?" Holder demanded, stalking over to stand

next to him.

"The Net!" he laughed, joy on his face. "It's open to everyone now, not just the Holders. The Prophecy Child, he opened the Net to everyone!" The Watcher laughed in wonder as he refocused and gazed at Holder.

Holder took a step closer to the ball of light, closed his eyes as the Watcher had. When he opened his eyes, he cried out, "I connected to the Net." Holder trembled. He thought, I have access to everything ever recorded, written down, not only on Upik, but on every planet. Data known to every species who'd ever linked to the Net, all of it, available now at the flash of a thought. "Interstellar Net connection," breathed Holder in wonder.

"Trillions of sentients on every planet are freely linked because of the Prophecy Child's gift," declared the Watcher. His eyes held triumph, perhaps even a bit of defiance directed at Holder.

Tears ran down Holder's face. He fell to his knees. "How could the Holder prophecy have been so wrong?" He wailed, blinking his eyes up at the Watcher. He gazed back at the hut where the child had been born. "If I had succeeded ..." he shuddered, feeling sick.

The Watcher put his hand on Holder's shoulder gently. "Take heart, your Holder Order did not succeed. Upik is no longer in the dark. We Watchers of the Quantum Block Sphere Temple have fought against you Holders for hundreds of years. At last we've succeeded. Our holy destiny was to bring our planet closer to the fabric of all that was, that is, and will be. To bring our planet closer to the great Creator."

"Would I find your creator in the Net?" asked Holder in a small voice.

"You can search," answered the Watchers softly. "But it is the Creator that finds you, if you but open your heart to space, and time, and all possibilities that is the Creator."

The Watcher walked away, quietly slipping into the dark.

For a long while, Holder still sat bent on his knees on the Gri-float staring at the hovering Net lights, contemplating how he could have been so wrong about everything he'd been led to believe for his whole life. But after a while, he realized he had an opportunity like none other before him. So Holder closed his eyes, and began his search for the Creator on the Interstellar Net, unfettered for the first time.

THE TWO-FACED MAN
BY
ROY BAIRD

"How can the past and future be, when the past no longer is, and the future is not yet? As for the present, if it were always present and never moved on to become the past, it would not be time, but eternity."
St Augustine, Confessions

Minds more learned than mine consider time to resemble a fourth dimension because three dimensional events occur as a conjoined sequence in our consciousness. Each event is a point. Yet they flow together as one. Whether this is true or not, it is a fact that we humans are confined to the present and can't skip backwards or frontwards in time. That would be untheological.

But I've also heard theologians expound to us that we mortals are allegedly constituted of body and spirit. If this is so, and I've no reason to deny it, I've often wondered whether our spirits are as bound by time as our bodies. And, after a few glass-shaped spirits of my own, I've sometimes speculated, while it is obvious our bodies are visible and our souls invisible, how our non-corporeal selves might reveal themselves in time. Because of a couple of events I've experienced that can only be explained by these two happenings taking place, I've since concluded that spirits can make themselves manifest and even travel through time.

Does that make the theologians right or wrong? You tell me. But I can tell you this. As a failed politician– and aren't we all?–

29

I've written this story as part confession, part manifesto. My declared intention is to present two pieces of evidence for the sincerity of my beliefs in this matter. They will take the form of two spiritual experiences that I trust will speak for themselves.

The first of these theological deeds occurred when I was about ten or eleven. It must have been a Friday for my mother had travelled into town to perform the weekly rite of grocery shopping and had gifted me some space of own. Before departing, she asked if I could fend for myself for an hour and promised to return as soon as the shops would decree. I hadn't felt at all well that morning. The night before had left me in a troubled and restless spirit, so my mother had rather grudgingly allowed me to take the day off school, despite the suspicion of malingering that all such occasions invoke.

Yes, I was eleven because I was vaguely aware that Winston Churchill had won the general election and was Prime Minister again at the age of seventy-six, two years younger than I am now. My interest in a political career was probably sparked around then too, as I listened to him speak on our family radiogram. I enacted an adequate impression of his oratory because family's friends used to give me twelve pence for impersonations. It is my political party trick, and one that symbolised the rest of my career. Shillings for speeches, shekels for shackles.

After mother left that morning, I'd tried to take my mind off my mental miseries by lying on my back and tracing imaginary outlines on the ceiling stains, then by counting the roses on the wallpaper. But as this hadn't helped, I decided to rise and roam around to help speed up the passage of time. My first stop was at the kitchen to pour myself an extravagant glass of water, which bored me almost immediately. Then I drifted into the sitting room at the front of the house and idly fingered the keys of our old piano. Tedium followed fifteen seconds later, and the window seemed to call out for my special attention.

As I looked outside, I was somewhat startled and stunned to see an elderly man standing at our gate, scrutinising our house and grounds with apparent interest. As I watched him, shielding my body behind a large musty curtain, my attention was drawn to his appearance more than his actions. His face seemed almost familiar, yet my memory told me that I had never met him before. And I was sure from his clothing that he wasn't from around our small, rural neighbourhood.

Before long he spied me looking out at him and as our eyes briefly convened, he appeared even more surprised to see me than I was him. I pulled back from the window with a jolt, annoyed that I had been spotted, but not before he'd granted me a small, hesitant wave. After waiting a few seconds, or minutes, I ventured a cautious peek out to see if the stranger was still there, but I was unable to locate him in the garden or at the gate. I pressed my face closer to the window in order to spread out a wider range of vision, hoping to see if perhaps he'd marched off down the road. But, by some miracle, he was nowhere in sight. This puzzled me mightily at the time, although I was not afraid.

I stepped away from the window. Yes, I was unafraid, but I did feel a small knot of uneasiness because of the incident. Yet this was cancelled out by another sensation. For in the short time that our eyes had locked together, there seemed to exist an affinity between the two of us, a sort of connection that I couldn't explain. At the time I found this baffling more than fearful. His presence hadn't perturbed me, but as to whom he was, or where he had gone, I had no idea. I departed back to bed and reflect on this strange encounter of a man at our gate who was both unknown and known at the same time, near and yet far. As I continued to mull this over in my mind, it suddenly became clear to me why the man's face had seemed recognisable. This I found hard to believe, yet it was true—he had borne a striking resemblance to my father!

I lay in prostrate on my bed to work out the implications of this revelation. If the window man truly looked like my father, then the only conclusion I could come to was that perhaps he was one of my father's brothers. My father was from a large family of fourteen children and I knew that he had several brothers. I had met most of them at one time or another, and I was almost certain that he wasn't one of them. But he may have had a brother that I hadn't yet met or about whose presence I was unaware.

To settle my soul, I resolved to ask my mother when she came home just how many brothers my father had and if any were about now, for I reckoned that she was bound to know. In the meantime, I tried to curb my impatience until then by involving myself once more in some time passing activities such as practising my political oratory and thinking of ways to make more money from it. But she seemed to take forever!

Then at last, to my relief, I heard the key in the door and my mum entering. Before she put away the shopping, she came into my bedroom to ask how I was feeling, which was timely for I was dying to ask her the questions that were on my mind. Yes, she was certain that my father did have several brothers, seven in fact. But no, she didn't think any of them were visiting here just now. Of course, she was curious to know why I wanted this information, so I told her that I was just interested and that was all, which seemed to satisfy her. I had no taste for telling her the truth, since she would think that if I was well enough to exit my bed and see strange visions, then I was well enough to attend school. Yet her answers hadn't shed any light on the identity of the mystery window man, so I was left wondering. To my delight she had bought me a comic and sweets, so immersing myself in these, the incident was temporarily forgotten.

Over the succeeding years this peculiar incident did cross my mind on occasion, but these got fewer as the inevitable cares and worries of life claimed my attention. I left school, worked six wearisome years as a clerk in an accountant's office, served six years in the army, found myself in a couple of middle management positions after that, and finally found time to dip my toes into the mucky waters of local politics. Along with this, I managed to marry, buy a house, father two sons, bury both my parents, and deal with all the connected responsibilities. My passion became politics, with its promises of power as a force for good and visions of a brighter future, just past the edge of sight.

At the same time, and to my amazement, I was subject to the ageing process like everyone else. My hair gradually turned grey and then white, my face developed lines and wrinkles, and my appearance slowly but surely changed from that of a young man to that of an elderly man who, without my fully realising it, bore a striking resemblance to my father. In fact, this was first brought to my attention at a relative's funeral, when some obscure relations whom I had never met before all agreed that they would have known who I was, for I looked so like him. This revelation had a strange outcome and one that struck me one day as I was shaving. Before, each time I looked in the mirror, I only saw the familiar face looking back, the face that bore a resemblance to my father. But now, bizarrely enough, and to my astonishment, I now saw the face of the man I'd seen all those years ago–the face of the window man!

As my body waned, so did my interest in politics. As a boy, I started out by acting Winston Churchill. But as a man, I grew bone-tired of acting out words, ideas, slogans and sentiments that weren't me. More often, rather than Churchill, I felt like Stalin instead, turning tragedies into statistics. There's only so much two-facedness a man can enact before he starts to lose a sense of his real self, his own soul. And how many votes will a man give in exchange for his soul? I learned at church one day that the word 'hypocrite' originally meant actor, a man with two faces, a mask of skin. And it struck me that I started out as an actor and, thanks to politics, I'd never stopped. What–or who–could liberate me from this impostor's syndrome?

Then the second of these spiritual occurrences took place which reminded me of the mysterious nature of life. Towards the end of my last term in the town council, I successfully reached the office of mayor. This required a move from my home village to a more central location. So, I decided one day to drive out and take a last look at the house where I was born and bred. After parking the car, I walked over the road towards the little cottage I once called home. It looked occupied and in a state of severe modernisation, but still recognisable, still mine. I stopped and stood at the gate, surveying the garden and grounds I once knew so well. There was the lawn that I cut every Saturday, the hedges that my father had kept so trim, and the bushes and the flower beds he had once tended, all still visible, although blurred with time and cement.

As my eyes drifted over this scene, strangely my mind went back to that day long ago when I had acted too sick to attend school and had looked out the window, that day I spied the man with the familiar face standing at our gate, looking over the house and grounds, just as I was doing now. As I thought of this, I instinctively eyed the window and was startled and surprised to see the face of a young boy looking out at me. At first, I thought that this was a mere coincidence and that he was one of the children of the family now living there, but as we eyed each other, I was astounded by the realisation that I had seen his face many times before. So flabbergasted was I by this, that I was momentarily taken aback. Not knowing what to do next, I gave him a little wave, at which he turned away from the window and disappeared. I momentarily remained at the gate, awestruck, before continuing my walk over the road, all the while mulling over what I had witnessed.

When I arrived home, in order to confirm what I'd seen, I brought down an old photograph album from a cupboard and leafed through its pages until I found the object of my search. There, sure enough, regarding me from an old black and white school photograph, was the face of a young boy aged between ten and eleven, with a strange haircut, and a dour expression. I compared it to other photos—the face of a man on his wedding day, a man with his two boys, a man at the end of a political career when all hope of change had changed to vague promises and self-promotion.

Over the years I'd looked at this photograph on numerous occasions, so the facial image was well-known to me. In fact, this knowledge had been what had made encountering that face at the window so unbelievable to me at the time, for not only was the face familiar, but I also knew whose face it was. That was the miraculous thing about it, and what I found so hard to believe, yet impossible not to know, for in the photograph was the very face of the window man, the face that was my own.

Or one of them.

Which one it was, I'll leave to the theologians. Politics creates such two-faced men as me. Something about politics, a pressure to pretend that we and the world appear other than what we are, a forcing of cities of men into the City of God, lies at the back of it. Maybe something beyond it can take those masks of ours away, so that someday the boy and the man in us, instead of missing the other, can stand face-to-face, reconciled, as friends. Maybe it's up to us.

Once upon a time, a man said that if the face is a politics, dismantling the face is also a politics. You can have a true face, or a two-face, but not both. The false face of political promise—coercion disguised as benevolence, tyranny wearing a mask of consent—must be wiped away. How? I don't yet know, but I believe in time it's possible. For, as I heard in the days of my unspoilt youth, the wolf shall dwell with the lamb, and a little child shall lead them.

MALICYDE ROTH, SALTWITCH INSURANCE INVESTIGATOR: THE ALIEN ARSON MATTER

BY

KAEDING SINDELAR

Malicyde Roth tamped a pinch of *tabák* into the bowl of her churchwarden pipe. Aromas of dried *kaffa* leaf, leather, and earthy woodland sage evoked the memory of her mother's kitchen table where she first learned how to add fire-salt in just the right proportion so as not to burn the blend. She slipped the tamping blade into her belt and brought the forearm-length pipe to her lips. She released a trickle of *život*–her inner life force–from her lips, blew it through the stem and into the pipe's bowl, igniting the fire-salt. She raised the hood of her saltwitch cloak against the cool, damp night and took a drag of warm smoke. A rush of the herbal stimulants made the freckles on her lavender skin sparkle like blinking fireflies at dusk and kept her alert in the wee hours before dawn.

For three nights, she'd been staked out on the roof of a boarding house across the street from Shanugl's Tavern. One of her informants had tipped her off that the jewel thief Rast Onetooth would be meeting his fence there to sell pieces he'd lifted from a wealthy widow after conning her into a romantic relationship. For three nights, Mal murmured prayers of good hunting to Rozměsíc–Goddess of the Shattered Moon–as she traversed a starry sky in the ancient chase of her spurned lover, the Sun. If only she could catch him, he might fuse the three pieces of her back together and heal her broken heart. But alas, she slipped over the horizon and once again the bells of Droig Temple rang out the sunrise hour.

"Sard," Mal cursed. Another wasted night spent on her own failed chase.

She tapped out the dregs from her pipe, stretched stiff muscles, and secured her wand in its holster, strapping it to her left thigh. She slung a leather satchel across her body, tucking it behind her. As she stowed her pipe, the tavern door opened and the servant boy stepped out. It was the same routine every morning. The boy would douse the streetlamp and then fetch a bundle of wood for the kitchen hearth. But this time he didn't put out the lamp and instead hurried down the side alley and disappeared into the shadows. When he reappeared, he wasn't carrying any wood and he wasn't alone. A tall lanky man shuffled behind him. The boy wrapped a staccato knock on the door and ran off down the street.

Mal reached back into her satchel's front pocket and pulled out a rounded lens like the type housed in a handheld magnifying glass. She cupped it between thumb and forefinger and held it up to her left eye. The lens was infused with light-bending salt and with a twist of her wrist, she pushed and pulled energy into and out of the lens, adjusting the optical magnification and focus. The door creaked open and Lanky Man turned into the lamplight. Mal increased the lens magnification and focused in on the man's face. His features generally matched the description of her thief, but there was no mistaking the one long snaggly tooth biting his lower lip.

Malicyde tightened the satchel strap and bolted to the rain spout set in the rooftop's corner. She flipped over the ledge and slid down the three story drainpipe. Her boots clattered on the cobblestone and she brushed off her hands on the backside of her cloak. The elderly landlady poked her head out the window, scowled and wagged a finger at Mal.

"Good morning Madam Hrevlicz. I apologize for the commotion, but you'll be pleased to know I won't be needing your rooftop for another night."

All wrinkle and snarl, Madam Hrevlicz snorted and hocked a gob of snot onto the street. "You pay for week. I have contract. No ree-fun!"

"I wouldn't dream of asking for a *refund,* madam." Malicyde twirled an exaggerated bow. "The overabundant warmth of your caring disposition would have been well worth twice the price."

"Hmrph." The old hag crossed her arms and angrily curled her horns tighter around her ears.

Mal leaned in closer and said, "Before I humbly depart, would you be so kind as to bestow one final service and go summon the constable?"

"At hour such as zis?" The madam's eastern mountain accent spat out each word like a disapproving scold. "No. Must make ready ze breakfast for husband." She stepped back and began to close the window.

Malicyde jammed her arm against the pane, a yellow paper cheque in her hand. The number one with the word "GOLD" underneath was printed in each corner and the logo of the *Second Community Bank of Hyanchar* was stamped in the center. Along the bottom edge an inscription read: *Redeemable for a weight of gold equal to one ludĕk gram. Purity of metals independently certified.* Mal said, "How rude of me. Perhaps this will–"

The piece of paper disappeared into the greedy nether regions of the crone's nightgown faster than her cooking made Master Hrevlic run for the outhouse. Without another word, the old woman threw on a woolen shawl and skittered out of the house. Her slippered feet crunched in the light snow that had begun to

fall, leaving tracks in the direction of Freith & Freith Constable
Company a few blocks away.

Mal grabbed her horns and twisted her head side to side,
cracking the tension out of her neck. She squared her shoulders,
threw open her saltwitch cloak and marched across the street.
She drew her wand, loaded *život* into it and pushed the life-force
out through the wand's shaft where it reacted with the crystalline
tip fabricated from pure *blesksůl*–"lightning salt" in the common
tongue. A jagged white-hot thunderbolt shot out from the wand
and blew the tavern door to smithereens. Mal leapt over the
gaping threshold and landed in a defensive crouch in the middle
of Rast, Shanugl and another man who were all on their hands
and knees, coughing on smoke and sawdust. She took out a letter
from her satchel and read, "From the *Judge Firm of Gryff, Raoul
and G'paj,* in accordance with the terms of his signed Contract of
Arbitration on file with the *Low Cost Guaranteed Insurance
Agency,* hereby issue a lawful arrest warrant for Rastrisj Ramcoff,
also known as Beanstalk Trisj, Rast Onetooth and Ram the
Comely–" Mal looked at Rast's snaggletooth. "Ram the Comely?
More like 'Damn He's Ugly.'" Mal chuckled, then continued, "–on
the charges of larceny, fraud, theft of property rightfully
belonging to blah, blah, blah." She flipped the warrant on the
floor in front of Rast and said, "You can read the rest at your
trial."

Rast staggered to his feet and pulled a knife from his boot.

Mal cocked her head. "Really?"

Rast lunged. Mal flicked her wand and hit him with a lower-
powered blast. He slammed backwards into the wall and
collapsed limp-bodied to the floor. "Anybody else?" The other two
men shook their heads and held up their hands. Mal rummaged
through Rast's coat pockets and pulled out a velvet bag.

"Hold it right there!"

Mal spun around and found a cocked flintlock aimed at her
chest, adroitly held by Liltyanj, the sister half of the Freith duo.

Her always dumbfounded brother stood beside her, fumbling at his holster strap.

"Mal?" The platinum haired sister lowered her rifle. "Of course it's you," she said and whacked her brother on the horn. "Leave your sarding pistol be, numbskull."

"Nice to see you too, Lilt," Mal said and tossed the lumpy velvet bag over to the brother. He flung out clumsy hands and clenched empty air. The bag hit him in the face. It fell to the floor and spilled out sparkling jewelry. The brother rubbed his nose and whistled.

Mal smirked. "Your timing is spot on as usual. Just in time to clean up my mess."

Malicyde propped open a window from her second floor apartment overlooking Commerce Street and let the smells of a waking Hyanchar City wash over her. Street vendors roasting *kaštan* nuts, exotic citrus fruits from the southern continent stacked up on carts, breads browning in ovens. It had taken over an hour to sort through the paperwork following the incident at Shanugl's tavern and she was hungry and tired. She cut slices off a block of cheese from her pantry, poured herself a glass of plum *slivo,* packed her pipe with her special relaxation *tabák* blend, and collapsed onto a pillowed bench by the window.

The *Crystalcomm* orb on her desk filled with smoke and chimed a repeating four-note melody. Mal's chest sank with a huff. She stretched and swiped her hand over the crystal ball. The chimes stopped and the swirling cloudiness inside the orb cleared away. She gulped down the *slivo* and burped out, "Malicyde Roth."

Within the orb, a warped image materialized of a stubby nosed woman with spiky gray hair and the signature horn piercings of one of the northern tribes. "Mal? It's Patrice McKraken of

Mercantile Mutual Insurance."

"Pat? Good grief word travels fast. How did you hear so soon?"

"Hear about what?"

"The Jaded Jewel Matter obviously. You know, the case I've been working on for you the past month? Now look, it's been a long night and a longer morning filling out the reports of the Constables Freith." Mal took a hit of her pipe. "It wouldn't have been so bad if it was just Lilt, but having to explain–*in triplicate*–to that halfwit brother of hers that what I did really wasn't wrongful assault and that Shanugl won't be pressing charges for property damage–well, *probably* won't be pressing charges."

"Wait, what! Mal what did you–"

"I'm sure whichever arbitration firm Shanugl uses will be more than happy to come to a discounted settlement. Hell, they may not even charge you for restitution considering the reputational damage they'll suffer once words gets out they've been representing someone who facilitates criminal activity on his business premises."

"Just a moment–"

"And I know, I know, as a representative of your company, it looks bad when I go around blowing up private property, even with a warrant. But what was I supposed to do? Would you rather pay a little gold in restitution to a crooked barkeep or let a thief get away and pay out the full jewelry insurance claim to your client? Look, if it makes you feel any better I didn't harm anyone."

"Mal, listen–"

"Well, I didn't kill anybody at least. Now Pat, it will all be in my expense report and I'll be happy to go over it in more detail with the arbitrator tomorrow, but I'm exhausted and need a couple more of these." Mal held up and waggled the empty glass.

"Malicyde Roth!"

Mal froze. If Pat was shouting her full name she must really be pissed. Pat cleared her throat and exhaled. "Look, I don't care about that now."

"Oh?" Mal put down her pipe and sat up. "Are you feeling alright, Pat?"

Pat rubbed her right horn anxiously. "I've got a top priority matter and I need you on it right away. *Top* priority."

Mal grinned. "Go on. And don't forget the part about my top priority bonus."

The cord connected to the bell above her apartment door vibrated, jingling the clapper. Malicyde strapped on her satchel and descended the stairs to first floor landing. She opened the door and a young lass, no more than fifteen years old judging by the slenderness of her horns, tipped her chauffeur cap and gave a slight nod. *"Faster Than Twelve Carriage Company* at your service, mistress. Take yer bag?"

"The bag stays with me."

"Aye, mistress." The chauffeur hustled to the carriage parked against the street curb, opened the passenger compartment door and lowered the footstep. The carriage, an older style of the kind pulled by horses before the invention of locomotive magics, had been converted for modern use which meant no need for slower horses and the accompanying smelly waste byproducts. Mal stepped in and took the forward-facing cushioned seat in the rear of the passenger compartment. The young driver secured the door and vaulted up to the driver's box attached to the front of the carriage. She thumped the back of her boot twice against the passenger car and called out, "Ready, mistress?"

Mal slid open the passenger window and hollered, "Half a *luděk* of gold if you get me there before noon!"

The girl grabbed the steering rod and squeezed out all the air in her lungs with a riotous "Hee yaw!" A torrent of raw *život* buzzed through the carriage and raised the hair on Mal's arms. The saltiron transmission squealed as the driver's energy surged into its gears. The wheels slipped once, twice, then caught traction. The carriage lurched forward and barreled down Commerce Street.

Mal took out a sheet of hemp paper from her satchel. The fibers had been infused with salt-ink during the paper's manufacture. She charged the sheet with *život* that mixed with the salts and catalyzed a reaction that instantly transcribed her spoken words onto the page:

> *Expense report for Malicyde Roth on behalf of the Mercantile Mutual Insurance Company in regards to The Alien Arson Matter.*
>
> *Case Summary: Insurance Agent Patrice McKraken explained that the largest warehouse of the Rivo Preservative Salts Company burned down and suffered a total loss of all contents. Because preservative salts prevent perishable foodstuffs from spoiling and aid in the modern manufacturing of durable goods–everything from carriage wheels to those new-fangled contraptions of the Crystalcomm Company's communication orbs–the total claim could be incalculable due to the negative effects rippling throughout the rest of the economy. Subsidiary insurance claims filed against Mercantile Mutual would be sure to follow. My assignment was to investigate the cause of the fire and to determine the full extent of liability for the company.*
>
> *Item 1: Twelve luděks of silver and four bronze for supplies at Havlicek's Apothecary and Conumdrium*
>
> *Item 2: Two and a half luděks of gold for transportation from my apartment in downtown Hyanchar to Rivoville, the homesteaded city of the Rivo Corporation. Usually two days travel by horse, Pat said to spare no expense and referred an upstart carriage company which she said had a fast driver. "Fast" was an understatement.*

The carriage swerved and drifted to a stop before the

smoldering remains of the warehouse. The chauffeur swooped down and opened the door. Mal stepped out and checked her pocket watch–barely quarter past eleven. "What's your name, lass?"

"Uhrayn, mistress."

Mal chewed the inside of her lip. "Is that Pallatian for 'jinx'? An odd name to say the least."

"Aye, mistress. Me parents was a superstitious lot. The name's meant to ward off bad luck, you see."

Mal flipped Jinx a gold coin. "The power of your *život* is impressive. Not many Djar can manipulate saltiron like that and those with your level of power usually get into high salaried industrial work."

The driver's freckles sparkled as she tugged her vest straight and stood tall. She patted the logo on the side of the carriage, beamed a wide grin and said, "Never was much fer bosses." The logo showed a horse painted with a number twelve running behind a carriage. "This here's all mine. Owns it outright, I do. Only have the one carriage now, but in a few years, I'll be able to expand. Build me a transportation empire, I will."

"I don't doubt it."

A stomp of footsteps grumbled the approach of angry men. The first wore jeweled horn-caps and a perfectly tailored suit composed of tan linen pants and a coat dyed in the signature crimson color of the Rivo Company with gold threaded cuffs. A step behind him followed an absolute hulk with bulging muscles on display through a sleeveless crimson tunic. Muscle-man sported no lavish affectations, only a raised scar on his left cheek that traced the curve of where his horn would have been had it not been broken off.

Mal addressed the better-outfitted of the preceding two. "Mr. Rivo, I presume?" Mal stepped forward and pressed her left fist to her chest. "The name's Roth, Malicyde Roth. I'm the insurance investigator."

The well-dressed Rivo stopped just short of pressing his nose against hers. He did not return the polite gesture of salutation. "This is a waste of time. Your employer is stonewalling. I need to be compensated for my loss. I've paid insurance premiums for twenty years and now when it's time to pay they send investigators to stonewall!"

Mal lowered her fist, but did not unclench it and did not step back. "I assure you that is not how I operate."

"Words are cheap," growled Rivo.

"Sir, if you're quite finished..." Mal pushed her cloak open and rested palm on wand. "I have a job to perform in accordance with your contract. Please move aside."

Rivo bit his lip, took a step back and spat on the grond. "Fine. But I already know who's responsible."

Mal motioned for Jinx to follow her into the center of the burned out warehouse remains. "Is that right?"

"That's right. It's one of those filthy human refugees from the western continent by the name of Taek Gin. I fired his lazy sarding ass a week ago and he burns my warehouse down in revenge."

Mal pulled out the magnifying glass and handed her satchel over to Jinx. She knelt over a burnt wood beam and twisted the lens back and forth, turning the wood over several times. "Scalpel."

After a moment, Mal looked up at Jinx's questioning face. Mal snapped her fingers twice, held out an open hand and nodded at the satchel. Jinx flipped open the briefcase sized satchel bag and rummaged around.

"Uh, there's a lot of...*stuff* in here. Seems like this bag should weigh at least twice as much," Jinx said. Her eyes widened and she stopped searching. She pulled out a hand-length sheath and laid it in Malicyde's palm.

Mal unrolled the sheath revealing a set of surgical knives. "Was it a guess?"

"Me auntie be a surgeon."

Malicyde lifted an eyebrow. "Fantastic." With one of the scalpels, she scraped off a bit of the ash from the wooden beam and stood up. She took out a vial from the satchel and tapped the ash into it. She grabbed yet another vial filled with a pink salt suspended in a clear solution, dribbled a few drops into the vial with the ash, shook it and held it up to the light. The ash changed from gray to blue to bright red.

"What are you doing?" Rivo demanded.

"A test for magical residue."

"And?"

"There's no doubt. Magic was used here," Mal said.

"I told you! It was the human. Humans and their dark occult blood magic. Look at their societies. No respect for our property with their unending wars and *go-ber-nenz*," said Rivo.

Mal's species the Djar, had no word for "government". Her people only learned of the concept a couple of decades ago when humans first sailed to the Djar continent.

"Why are you so sure it was this Taek?" Mal asked.

"Now you're asking the right question." Rivo waved the muscular man over. "Show her, Nuel."

By the look of him, Nuel's muscles would keep him moving long after his brain stopped working so a head shot might be out of the question if she ever got into a fight with him. Nuel opened up a canvas sack and pulled out a fist sized chunk of fire-salt crystal. Jinx whistled. Fire-salt was one of the most sought after substances known and its power was matched only by its scarcity.

Nuel grunted out, "I find in quarters. Under bed of Taek."

"Not from around here are ya, big fella?" Jinx asked.

Mal shot Jinx a glare and she backed up towards the carriage. "I imagine a pure block of crystal like that would be worth more than a month's wages. Why would this Taek fellow leave it behind?"

"Who knows why humans do anything. Now you've seen the

evidence. Go write your report and tell your boss to pay me my insurance money!" Rivo pulled out an envelope from his vest and shoved it in the Nuel's hands. "Go to Judge Ramskinj. Get an arrest warrant and a posse. Taek is going to get what he deserves."

Mal walked back to the carriage and pulled Jinx aside. "How'd you like to earn another ten *ludĕks?*"

"Silver?" The girl raised slightly on her toes.

"Gold."

"Holy sard!" The girl's face flushed chartreuse and she averted her eyes. "Apologies for the foul language, mistress." Jinx snapped to attention. "Faster Than Twelve Carriage Co is at your service, mistress!"

"Good. I've got a special mission for you, but first take me to the CrystalComm office in town." Mal stepped onto the carriage and paused. "Never was much for sarding niceties." The saltwitch winked. "Call me Mal."

Expense report continued...

Item 3: Two ludĕks silver for a long-distance orb-call to Patrice McKraken letting her know the latest developments. Rivo said that this human Taek would likely be found hiding out at one of the churches that assisted refugees. I had the carriage driver drop me off at a church run by a Father Gik, who I knew from a previous investigation. I hoped he could provide a lead–for a small donation, of course.

Item 4: Ten ludĕks gold for continued carriage service and to send the driver on a potentially dangerous assignment. I only hoped she could get there in time.

Item 5: Two ludĕks silver for a donation to the church. I knew the priest there, Father Gik, and hoped he could give me a lead on the human.

"Malicyde Roth! May my eyes fall out should they deceive me! The mighty saltwitch mingling with us downtrodden? How can this be? There's no bonus in it."

Father Gik was short and pudgy with the palest lilac-colored skin Mal had ever seen. He wore long sleeves even on a warm sunny day for risk of burning his skin.

Mal looked the priest up and down, but mostly down. "Nice to see you as well Gik. Although I never thought you'd end up a priest. Too short to reach heaven."

They stood in silence for a moment and then laughed. Gik slapped Mal on the arm and said, "Please join us for the evening meal."

Father Gik's church wasn't much more than a two-story wood barn surrounded by a series of smaller dormitories on a few homesteaded acres of land. Gik ushered her inside, passing rows of humans of all ages laid out on blankets or praying together in circles. Many of the children kept company with the elderly near the pit fires in the corners.

Mal tugged the priest's tunic and leaned in close. "What's going on here?"

Gik stopped beside a young woman with blue eyes, long brown hair tied in a single braid, and skin so pale Mal wondered if such a person could ever go out into the sun. The priest bowed over her and uttered some words in the human tongue which Mal did not understand, but by the cadence seemed to be a blessing of some sort. Gik turned back to her and said, "They're refugees. They come from a land where they slave under barbaric government rule. Drafted into armies and forced to murder their neighbors to steal scarce resources rather than trade for them."

"And you take care of them." Mal said matter-of-factly.

"All of God's creatures deserve our grace." Gik bent down, whispered something in a gray haired man's ear and patted him on the shoulder. After walking a few more paces, Gik said, "That man lost three sons and a daughter in war. Yet, still he summoned the strength to cross the great sea. For life. For freedom. My faith calls me to help them."

Against the wall, a little girl missing a leg lay on a straw mat and coughed violently while she slept. *What strength of faith did it require to come this far?*

Mal shook tears away and said, "I'm looking for a man named Taek Gin."

Gik bent down and wiped spittle from the girl's mouth. "The warehouse fire." Gik looked over his flock and sighed. "I suppose trying to hide him from you will be useless."

A gong rang out. People streamed into the hall and sat cross-legged on mats in rows along low tables. Gik stepped up on a dais in the center of the room, raised his arms and bowed his head. "Let us pray. Goddess Rozměsíc, protector of the broken, please bless this meal we are about to receive, that it may nourish our souls and give us strength to continue your work to bring harmony among all peoples, human and djar."

Gik clapped three times and the congregation sang a singular long note in response. Children brought out bowls of thin soup and hunks of bread. A young man with a shaved head and bronze skin sat next to Mal. Gik clasped him on the shoulder. "Mal. Meet Taek."

Taek held out his hand. Mal shot a questioning look at Gik. The priest grabbed Mal's hand and clasped it with the human's. "They call it a handshake. It's a form of greeting."

After a moment they broke their grip and Mal said, "Tell him I'd like to share my pipe with him."

Mal pulled out the churchwarden from her cloak, tamped in a pinch of *tabák*, sprinkled a little extra fire-salt on it and took a puff. She handed it to Taek which he put to his lips and waited. He looked at Mal, pointed to the pipe bowl repeatedly, then spoke a single word which Gik translated as "candle".

"Attention! Attention! This is an announcement of the Traej

Gunslingers Union." Mal drew her wand and ran to the open door. Five people dressed in tan uniforms emblazoned with the logo of the bounty hunter company, stood in a semicircle, each with their hands on the pistols at their hips. Rivo stood behind them. A man in the center held a metal megaphone and hollered, "We apologize for the interruption, but we have a lawful warrant of arrest to serve and will compensate you for your cooperation!"

Translations rippled through the crowd of parishioners and panicked voices grew into a loud cacophony. Gik waved his arms up and down, swiveling around. "Quiet everyone. Quiet. It's alright."

Mal stepped out, released a slow building charge into her wand, but didn't let it go. Megaphone-man pointed to the water tower behind him. "I'd think twice about that. Your reputation precedes you Miss Roth and I have no doubt that you might be able to dispatch us all before we got off one shot. But no way you'd beat my sharpshooter."

Mal looked up and saw the rough shape of someone with a rifle perched on the water tower landing. Father Gik and a few of his followers ran up beside Mal.

"My name's Jel. I have in my possession a lawful warrant signed by the honorable Judge Ramskinj for the arrest of one human male by the name of Taek Gin. Charged with the crime of arson and endangerment of life. He is to stand trial in three days, but may raise bail."

Mal lowered the wand to her side, but kept the charge building. "He didn't do it."

"That's for a jury to decide Miss Roth. Now stand down." He tipped his hat. "Please."

Father Gik stepped forward and said, "My flock walks a peaceful path. But we will resist if we must in the name of justice."

Jel shook his head. "I am justice."

The gunslingers drew their pistols.

Rivo shouted, "You know he's guilty! You saw the evidence!" He slapped the gunslinger on the back. "Do your job."

As the gunslingers moved in, Mal raised the hood of her cloak covering her face, and when they were half a pace away, released the charge from her wand into the ground. An eruption of earth flew up and out, knocking everyone one off balance. Mal rushed past the line of gunslingers and grabbed Rivo from behind, putting her wand against his temple.

"Call it a day's work or your employer loses his head."

Jel rubbed a speck of dirt from his eyes. "Miss Roth. Consider what you're doing."

A rifle shot rang out from the water tower catching Mal in the leg. She dropped her wand and collapsed to the ground. The gunslingers ran towards her. A carriage appeared from behind Mal skidding to a halt inches from crushing her and provided cover from the sharpshooter.

Jinx jumped down and rolled on the ground, swooping up the wand. She grabbed Mal under the armpit and stood her up facing the gunslingers. "Don't move ye scoundrels!" Jinx fired a warning shot over their heads.

Rivo crawled away on his belly and Jinx put a boot in his back. "Where do ya think you're goin'?"

Mal leaned against Jinx on one foot. "Did you get it?"

Jinx smiled.

Father Gik ran to her side. "Mal, are you alright? There's no need to fight. The goddess will protect us."

"Don't worry Father." Mal opened the door to Jinx's carriage and pulled out a middle-aged man dressed in a judge's robe. "This is the not so honorable Judge Ramskinj. My assistant beat Rivo's muscle man Nuel to the judge's office–she's a real fast driver, you see–and delivered this letter to the judge." Mal held up the parchment. "But the judge didn't have time to open it before Nuel arrived. Had he, he would have seen that the letter was blank, for unbeknownst to him, was infused with ink-salt. Nuel, on orders from Rivo, bribed the judge into issuing a false warrant and the whole transaction was recorded on this paper."

"Lies!" cried Rivo.

"Yes, there have been many lies, Mr. Rivo. Like the one about the fire-salt."

Rivo turned to the gunslinger leader and ordered, "Don't just stand there like an idiot! Arrest her!"

Jel looked at Mal and said, "Go on."

Mal limped over to Jel and handed him the parchment. "The human Taek Gin has been accused of arson by using fire-salt magic. Yet, when I offered him my pipe, he was unable to light it. He has no magical powers. In fact, no human I've ever encountered does. It's a common stereotype."

Rivo's face turned a shade of angry pink. "You said it yourself that the fire was caused by magic. This is ridiculous."

Mal hobbled forward and put her nose in Rivo's face. "No, I only said that magic had been used there. But the magic residue I recovered from the arson remains could not have survived a fire. It was a hoax placed after the fact to make it seem like fire-salt magic had been used to start the fire." Mal turned to the judge. "How much money did Nuel bribe you with for the warrant?"

The judge started to sob. "It's true. I'm so ashamed."

"No!" Rivo pushed Jel off balance, grabbed his gun, aimed it point blank at Mal and cocked the hammer.

Jel punched Rivo in the face, knocking him down. "Mr. Rivo. I regret to inform you that you have violated the no fraud clause of your contract. I hereby dissolve said contract and place you under arrest." He bent down and cuffed him. "There will be no refund."

Jinx helped Mal hobble into the passenger compartment, the wound in her leg throbbing. Jinx leapt into the driver's box and thumped her boot against the car. "Hold on, Mal!"

Malicyde grinned. On the way out of town, they passed the boarded-up office of the disgraced Judge Ramskinj, a bankruptcy notice nailed to the door.

Expense report summary of the Alien Arson Matter submitted for reimbursement to the Mercantile Insurance Company:

Pat, you'll be happy to know that I have concluded that your company has no liability for the warehouse fire. After further investigation assisted by Jel the Gunslinger, we uncovered evidence that Rivo had run the company into the ground and that there was nothing in the warehouse at the time of the fire other than worthless scrap. The insurance scam was a last ditch effort to save his business. I figure he and the judge will be spending quite some time in debtor's prison.

On a personal note, humans may be aliens in our land, but Father Gik showed me that compassion combined with faith, can build a bridge bringing our two species together through liberty and peace. Unlike magic, those ideals are within us all.

Total expenses as itemized on the attached supplemental ledger: thirty five luděks gold and twelve bronze.

Yours Truly,

Malicyde Roth

THROUGH THE FIRE
BY
M. ALLYSON SZABO

In October 1553, the Jewish people of Venice were living in the Venetian Ghetto, a tiny corner of the famous city. It was the first named Ghetto, designed both as a place of segregation and of protection. Travel in and out of the Ghetto was strictly controlled, and Jews could only leave during daylight hours. Still, the Jews thrived in their small enclave. They created businesses, Synagogues, and ran their own printing press. Then, Pope Julius III, seeing an offense to Christianity within the Talmud, ordered the destruction of the Hebrew writings. The Doge of Venice sent priests to the Ghetto, where hundreds of Jewish texts were thrown into the square and burned.

Antonia watched Pietro from the shadows, one pale hand against the cool brick of the building, the other holding her veil in place over her face. He was so passionate! Yet he was a Jew, the son of a moneylender. The Jews were outsiders, of course, confined to the ghetto, less than human. His faith was strong, though, she could see that. He radiated strength of spirit, even though he was not Christian. And he was beautiful, despite being older. He would make a phenomenal guardian, she had decided, a servant of God and a protector of man. Tonight, she would speak to him, convince him to become one of the guardians of Venice.

Pietro had no idea he was being observed, as he stood in the main square, watching the flames rise higher and higher. The heat was blistering, reddening his face as he shifted closer and closer. He had tucked his hair up into the red hat that was the required mark of a Jew within the borders of Venice. The pile of precious books was burning into holy ash, ash that marked his face as his tears left streaky tracks down his cheeks.

Antonia hung on his words as he muttered another prayer in Hebrew. He dashed forward once more, trying to rescue one of the books, a single precious book of the Talmud or Torah to carry forward. The Word of God burned before him, and his heart hammered in his chest from the horror of it all.

Antonia savored that heartbeat. It was strong, and echoed above the other sounds in the expansive square. As the flames danced and the pages of flowing Aramaic script burned, she wondered if this dark eyed, somber man could love her with the depth that she loved him. There were dozens of other humans in the plaza, all oblivious to her presence. Some wandered aimlessly and others stumbled by, sometimes sobbing, other times shrieking of coming doom. The darkness hid her slight form, and special prayers protected her from their gaze regardless.

Her fingers played across the glass bead at her throat which was anointed with her own blood. It was the recipient of the protection prayer which kept her hidden from human eyes. When she had died and been reborn, one of the blessings she had been gifted with was the ability to use blood to hide herself and others. A drop of blood, a spoken prayer, and a holy sigil sketched in the air, and none of the humans could see her. It was a useful talent, and allowed her to move among the streets and canals of Venice without concern.

Most of those she could see in the plaza were Jewish, but a handful of Christians looked on. They made sure that the Jews didn't rescue their literature from the purifying flames. A loud clatter stole her attention as a nearby canvas awning collapsed in flames. Several of the onlookers kicked it into the pile of burning books, away from other things that might burn. Antonia used the distraction to dart several doorways over, toward Pietro. She sought to be closer to that loud, pumping heart, as her own blood sang in unison with his.

A priest tossed handfuls of bound pages onto the already large pile as Pietro stood there. He drew back, almost until his back touched the wall of the building Antonia was crouching beside. She hitched her veils into place, practiced fingers pinning them so they would not fall if she had to run. She reached out to him, ready to snatch him and carry him away from the inferno before them.

She was about to grab and subdue him when he rushed forward, an anguished cry ripping from his smoke damaged lungs. Her hands flew to cover her mouth, stifling her own scream as he plunged into the flames. What was he doing? In the name of all that was holy, was he sacrificing himself? No, he was coming out now, covered in ash. The fire was licking demonically at his clothing, his hair, and his body.

Clutched to his chest was a single tome, singed only at the edges. Antonia shook her head, tears in her eyes. The priests hadn't seen him because of the thick black smoke that was now billowing out of the pile. Pietro made it three steps before falling to his knees, choking on the acrid vapors filling his lungs. He collapsed to the cobblestones, book still grasped in a death grip. Antonia listened intently as his heart skipped a beat, tried to continue, then stopped.

She had no more time to make her decision. There was no time to ask him what he wanted. If she would save him, she needed to do it immediately. She waited only a half a breath then darted out of the shadows and snatched the arm of his coat. He was larger than her, not by much, though he was a lot heavier. Her prayers and faith gave her strength, and she dragged him into a darkened walkway south of the square. She smothered the remaining flames and embers, listening all the while for his heartbeat. She heard nothing.

With a soft sigh and a glance around to be certain they were alone, she leaned over his prone body and bit into his neck. The hot gush of his blood suffused her mouth, and her eyes shut with the ecstasy of it. She had dreamed of this moment for months, the eroticism of his vital force filling her. She hadn't fantasized about making him like her, though. She hadn't dared. Now, there was no choice. She flipped him to his back and pried open his mouth, then bit her own wrist, letting her blood drip into his mouth.

For the long span of ten or twelve breaths, nothing happened. There was only the furor of the abused Jewish people in the nearby square, and the occasional skitter of one of the ever-present rodents. She watched him, lips pursed into a thin line, desperate for it to work. She'd seen it done, but had never created another one like her before. Her own maker was gone, somewhere else in the world, and the only other revenants she knew were worshipers of Satan. She had no dealings with them and their infernal celebrations, their indiscriminate killing.

And then it happened. A twitch. That was all the confirmation she required. Antonia scanned the area around her once more, not with eyes alone, but with all senses extended. She heard and felt nothing, and suspected all attention was on the burning holy texts behind her. She scrambled to her feet, then lifted Pietro's bulky body as if he were a child. Embracing him tightly, the hard cover of his precious holy book pressed against her chest, she sprinted into the night.

There was only one official way to enter or leave the ghetto, and that was the filigreed bridge to the north. That was for humans, though, and she was not one of them anymore. Pietro's limp form was awkward, but not beyond her ability to carry. At the canal edge, she peered up and down, looking for boats or watchful eyes. Seeing none, she gathered herself, silent and stealthy. She launched in a silent arc of orange silk, her veils fluttering around her diminutive form. Her landing was graceful despite her full arms. She sprinted, putting as much space between her and the ghetto as possible.

She paused only once, several blocks away from the square, long enough to speak the prayers of hiding that masked her from others. She included Pietro in her prayers this time, smearing his filthy, blistered forehead with a line of her own blood. It glowed for a second, and then sunk into his flesh. She marveled in the powers that God had seen fit to give her, then ran south again, away from the noise and chaos.

Her current home was west of the big market, and the pathway took her through areas that were not populated. She skirted the lantern-lit broad streets and the darkness. She always stuck to the shadows, glad of the clouds obscuring the moon that night. Pietro sagged against her, unmoving, but she knew that would change. She must get him to her home before morning, ensconced in safety. Then she would bide her time.

Once she had passed the Bascillica del Frari, she knew she was safe. Still, Antonia never let her guard down. It wasn't until she had entered into the dark confines of her brick home that she let out a loud breath of relief. She bolted the door tight behind her, then placed Pietro's body onto the tile floor. With inhuman speed, she closed and locked every shutter and doorway, securing herself and Pietro within. Only then did she return to him, and carry him down a set of stairs to the canal-level crypt below.

Antonia's home was like all homes in Venice, a wooden platform that rested atop piles driven deep into the lagoon mud beneath. The brick above was well supported by the foundation, strong and sturdy. The lower level of her home contained a dock for the barges necessary for travel through some parts of the city. Her dock area doubled as a crypt. A walkway led to several small, floating barges decorated in black silks and brocades.

As she always did, Antonia took a moment to say her prayers before stepping onto her own funeral barge. She thanked God for bringing her through death to eternal life, and for granting life to Pietro. She considered laying him beside her, but felt that might be inappropriate. He was a Jew, after all. She chose one of the other barges, installing him on the rich, dark fabric with great care. She whispered the one short Hebrew prayer that she had learned, and blessed his charred body as best she could. With great reverence, she covered him with a sheer, dark silk then retired to her barge and to sleep.

Hours later, when the sun had risen and fallen and darkness had returned, Antonia awoke. She checked on Pietro, then scurried off to clean and dress herself, and to prepare clothing and sustenance for him. She knew he would awaken hungry, and that eventuality must be prepared for.

She pored over all the things she knew about the Jews. She couldn't provide a Rabbi to bless the donor, but perhaps she could find a Jewish woman? Thinking that over, it made little sense. It would make more sense that the thrall be a Gentile woman rather than a Jew. The Jews had a prohibition on harming other Jews. Though it might not matter at all. She pursed her lips together, frustrated with her lack of knowledge.

The chosen thrall was a girl who couldn't have been more than seventeen. Her dark curls were modestly covered by a lacy white veil. Antonia led the young Christian into her home, once again locking all the doors behind her. "Pietro is new, and therefore may be clumsy. I will make certain no harm comes to you, regardless."

"Yes, Contessa." She bowed her head in acquiescence, keeping her eyes lowered.

Antonia could sense Pietro's faint stirrings below. She hurried the young woman down the cold stone steps and into the lower level. Pietro had not yet surfaced from the day sleep, but it was imminent.

"Wait here," she cautioned the girl and stepped onto the barge upon which Pietro lay. She gazed at his handsome face, barely obscured by the funerary cloth and no longer blistered or burned. She reached out, hesitant, her fingers aching to caress the curve of his cheek.

With a suddenness that left her gasping, he snatched her hand before it could reach his face. He sat up, the silk slithering off his body like a dark river. There was silence for several long moments, and then Pietro's emotionless eyes moved from Antonia to the young woman. The thrall crouched against one of the brick arches, unspeaking. Pietro's nostrils flared, and all his muscles became taut as he prepared to spring.

Antonia had anticipated this. The early hunger was sometimes overwhelming, and instinct took over no matter the faith and strength of the individual. Rebirth into afterlife was never easy. She had seen so many who, being risen again through the power of faith, had given over to the evil of the world. Such slaughter would never happen while she existed, not with her own progeny. Her hands wrapped around Pietro's upper arms, locking him into place.

A low growl erupted from him, a chesty sound that left her shivering. She expected him to attempt to throw her off, but he did not. He sat, fuming with restrained anger, but also observing.

"The girl is here to help you," Antonia offered, her voice quiet but intense. "She will help dull the hunger. But you must reach into the depths of your soul, and you must not give in to the evil that calls you to cause harm. Fight it, with every strength that God has given to you!"

"I don't understand," he croaked, one hand going to his throat. Antonia released him, but remained vigilant. His other hand still clung to the volume of the Talmud he had saved from the previous night's fires. He stared at the book, letting it settle into his lap. His fingers traced over the meticulous Hebrew letters on the cover. His grief was palpable.

"You need to eat," Antonia urged. "It will seem wrong, at first. But I assure you, the girl has agreed to this. You may question her yourself. It will be alright. I will help you."

Dazed, unsure of himself, Pietro slid off the barge and onto the walkway. His eyes flicked over everything, taking it all in. The young woman's heartbeat echoed in his ears, drawing him in, but he fought the animal instinct that clawed at him.

Antonia took the time to explain the process of eating to him in great detail. She warned him that if he didn't stop himself, she would do so.

"Do what you must," he whispered, unsure of his own soul at this moment. Nothing made sense, and his senses were going mad. He could hear everything, and it took great willpower to move slowly and with purpose.

He leaned toward the girl's exposed neck, breathing in the scent of her. He could see the heartbeat there, matching the reverberating drum in his head. For the first time, he felt his teeth elongate, becoming fangs. With a desperate, famished shudder, he bit down into the soft flesh. The girl moaned, and his own voice echoed hers as her blood welled in his mouth. He sucked it down in great gulps, overtaken by the sheer magnitude of what he was doing.

The animalistic nature of the act was about to overtake him, when Antonia's soft, feminine hand touched his shoulder. With a tortured cry, he pulled away from the girl, stopping himself.

"Lick the wound and it will heal." Antonia nodded as he did so, watching his amazement as the gaping holes closed up as if they had never existed. She then took the gasping and faint woman from him. "Wait here," she requested, and removed the woman from her home.

When Antonia returned, Pietro was sitting on the wooden walkway, touching his own teeth. The whites of his eyes showed, exposing his fear and concern.

"What am I?" he demanded immediately.

She lowered herself to sit beside him. "You are resurrected," she explained. As he protested, she held up a hand. "Not in the sense of the Christian faith. You are no longer living, but through your faith and the blessings of God, you have died and returned. It is possible for your death to cause you harm, and so for that reason you must hold tight to your faith. Faith protects us, and keeps us holy."

"I was burned," he stated, staring at his free hand. "But I saved this part of the Talmud. I walked into the flames."

"Yes, you did. And you died. Your heart stopped. But I couldn't let you die forever. You are an exceptional man. And so I took a little of the blood which is the blessing of my faith, and passed it into you, and so you were reborn. In doing so, it healed you of your wounds, and restored you."

He nodded, looking at the tattered, smoky clothing he was wearing, and the clean, pale flesh beneath. "You say God did this."

Antonia nodded. "The power is passed along among us. But it is the blessings of God Himself that sustain us and keep us strong. Those who fail, who lose their faith or never had faith to begin with, become *lamia*. They slaughter the innocent. We who hold onto our faith, who continue to worship God faithfully, who use our powers and abilities for the good of mankind, we are not *lamia*, but disciples. We are the resurrected."

Pietro shook his head and laid the book on the wood beside him. "The girl, I could hear her heart. But I cannot hear yours. Or my own."

"That's correct. Your heart no longer beats. You are now sustained by God, and by the kindness and sacrifice of others, rather than by your internal blood. You will sleep during each day, and walk the night. You will protect your people, and all peoples. I will teach you."

"What will you teach me?" He tilted his head, watching her. He fought with his conscience which told him that being alone with a Gentile woman was wrong, that drinking blood was wrong. Something within told him that this was as it should be, no matter how wrong it looked from the outside. Her words rang true. And so he listened.

She lit up like a candle. "I will teach you about our speed and prowess. I will teach you how to get sustenance without endangering the life of the humans you take from. I will teach you how to gain consent from them, and how to cause them no harm. I will teach you to blend into the night, so that you can stand up for the innocent and abused of Venice. I will teach you to fight for God, to destroy the *lamia* who kill indiscriminately."

"And who taught you?"

Her face fell. "The one who made me is long gone," she replied. "She was a wonderful, faithful woman. The crimes of the city wore her down, leaving her bereft and full of melancholy. She went east some years ago."

They sat in the dark for several minutes, listening to the sound of the water lapping against the wooden walkways and the barges.

"Who are you?" His gaze pierced her soul, and she shifted in discomfort from the intensity of it.

"I am Contessa Antonia Foscari, and I am a messenger and warrior of God. I am a good woman of Venice, and have lived here all my life, and my afterlife. I was born in Venice in the Year of Our Lord 1485, and I passed through the veil and was resurrected some twenty years ago. I am one of a handful of guardians of Venice. I devote my afterlife to helping those who need it, thanks be to God for preserving my soul and body." Her voice was clear, and she took a deep breath, and let it out slowly. She never took her eyes off him.

For his part, Pietro said nothing. He sat there, unmoving, a troubled look on his face. Finally, he spoke. "Did I kill that woman?" He rubbed one hand over his hair, and discovered that his red hat had disappeared somewhere in the previous night's flight. "And where is my hat? I require my hat."

Antonia laid one finger on his arm. "We will replace your hat, should you wish to continue wearing it. You can haunt the dark corridors of the canals, if you prefer, and not wear one. You only need the hat if you intend to show yourself as a Jew in the streets. And the woman is fine. We drink their blood, yes, but we do not harm them. There are some who do, certainly. Evil abounds, as always, and we must fight against it, as always. We, however, do not kill. I have watched you for months, from the shadows. You are a fierce protector of your people's literature and ways. You watch after them. The other Jews say some day you may be a Rabbi, which I understand is a great teacher, and somewhat like a priest."

"Not exactly, but I suppose the comparison is close enough. And how can you be sure I will not rampage and cause mayhem?"

"I have watched you, as I said. I know how you are seen among your people. But you are correct, travelling past the veil and into the afterlife is harrowing. There is always a chance you could turn to a darker path. If such a thing were to happen, I would be forced to kill you, as I kill any *lamia* who murders within Venice." She tugged on her veils, tucking them neatly in a nervous way. "I do not believe you will rampage, though. It does not fit your personality."

"You say you will teach me. I sense that this is a true statement. And yet, I find myself confused. You are a woman, and a Gentile woman at that. Yet I think it would be the height of hubris if I weren't to accept your offer of education."

"Perhaps you can also teach me," Antonia suggested, her tone meek.

"Perhaps. What do you wish to learn?"

"To read!" she blurted out. Her small hands grasped her skirts tightly. "I desire to read."

"In what language?"

She blinked. "I suppose in Venetian, although there are other languages I could learn."

"You implied that we have more than one life worth of time to spend. Education is always ongoing. It is an imperative of God. If you would learn to read, then I can teach you, though it is unusual for a woman to ask for this. I suppose it's even more unusual for me to be willing, but tonight seems to be a night for the unusual."

Antonia and Pietro had much to teach one another. She learned to read, as he promised. He was a patient teacher, and also an avid student, she discovered. He learned to use prayers and holy symbols to manipulate blood, in order to protect the Ghetto and its people. Together, they worked to keep safe the city of Venice, and all those who inhabited it. Christian, Jew, Muslim, heathen, they protected them all.

It was not easy work, nor was it always pleasant. And yet it fulfilled them. They became free, themselves, and they sought to gift that freedom of mind and person to all who they met.

THE REPENTANT SINNER
BY
SHASHI KADAPA

It rained that night. Thunder and lightning rent the dark sky, lighting the street in flashes. Ominous dark clouds shed rain in torrents that flooded the alleys. Electricity went off when it rained in Dharwad, and navigating the flooded streets in darkness was left to the brave and the stranded.

Vishwa Murthy Acharya or Acharyaru as he was called respectfully by the devotees at ShriRaghavendra Swami Matha temple looked apprehensively at the fury of Varuna, the rain god. He lit a kerosene lamp. The light flitted dimly across the dark corners of the pooja room.

Acharyaru peered in dismay at the clutter in the room. Sighing wearily, he bent to pick up the sacred pooja vessels, swept up flower offerings, and kept the Holy Scriptures in their place.

He was tired. As he rubbed his back, he muttered. All he wanted in life was to die with dignity and honour. The stone idol before him stared back in silence.

At nearly seventy, the daily rituals wore him out. The cold water baths in the morning, fasting until noon, constant rising and squatting during pooja made his knees tremble.

Acharyaru was short, stocky and his flesh sagged under the arms and belly. His attire was an old yet clean dhoti with his sacred thread the Janwaar looped around his shoulder and chest. With sandalwood paste smeared on his forehead, arms and chest, he was easily recognised when he went around the town. Simplicity, piety, honour, and respect characterised Acharyaru.

He glanced at the windows of the room. The only things that worked here were the broken windows with their shattered panes. They allowed the cold rain and the colder draughts to weave into the room, biting him like a wasp and making him shiver. Even worse, the draught tried to douse the holy diya that nevertheless continued to flicker in spite of the gusts.

Acharya had a tough time shielding the flickering flame, adjusting a thin shawl around his shoulders and chanting prayers. Mosquitoes buzzed around him, drawn by his warm flesh and the dark corners of the room in which he had spread the now wet rags to absorb the rainwater seeping from the roof.

At times like this he thought of his wife Savitri who had passed away a few years back. He had wept as he lit the funeral pyre. She stood with him in difficult times only to leave him all alone in his old age. This is nothing but Karma and there is no way to escape it. His time had not come yet.

The matha was his constant worry. He was a Brahmin priest and took pride that it was established a hundred years back. In the old days, people thronged the temple, especially on Thursdays, the favourite day of his Lord. To fulfil rituals, they offered gifts that he used to feed the devotees. His needs were simple, just food and Rayaru, the Swami to whom he offered prayers. Now people had turned to pseudo god men on TV who gave meaningless sermons, charged hefty amounts for a darshan, a consultation, and to answer a few questions. The times and people had changed while he remained what he was, a pious and poor servant of his Lord.

Not even one of his four sons was interested in continuing the priestly tradition, and this worried him.

"No Appa," they cried derisively, "we do not want this hard life."

Following the rigorous rituals, leading a morally upright life, fasting, and penance was hard. He shuddered to think of what would happen when he became too old and infirm to worship. *Would at least one of them turn to worship, Oh Raghvendra!*

❖

The next afternoon after his rituals, Acharyaru wearily sat on the steps of the decrepit rambling house where his extended family lived. He peered inside a couple of times and coughed, hinting for a glass of milk.

After some time, his grandson Arjun came with a full glass of milk. Arjun was his favourite and they often played together. The other grandchildren thought him old and did not like his dhoti that smelt of rancid butter. When they were young, he held them spellbound with stories from the Mahabharata, the Ramayana, and the ancient Puranas. Now all they wanted was TV, video games, and mobile phones.

"Where is Santosh?" He asked. Santosh was his youngest and favourite son.

"He has gone to college on his motorcycle", said Shanta, his second daughter-in-law.

"Ha, motorcycle! Why does he not ride a bicycle or go by bus? He wears pants, shirts, not a Dhoti."

"No one goes on a cycle, even girls ride scooters. And Dhoti? Even labourers do not wear them nowadays."

Of late, Acharyaru's daughters-in-law had begun answering back, sometimes questioning his authority, giggling and insulting him. They had begun to dislike the cloistered and strict regime and wanted freedom.

However, Acharyaru's family was the guardian of the temple and a high standard of behaviour were expected. During his weekly expositions of the puranas, he spoke about virtuousness, high moral standards, and about refraining from sins of the flesh and spirit. The tragedy was that his family did not pay heed.

One morning after the pooja, he had heard murmurs from among the devotees.

"Acharyaru should first teach his family about morals."

"I saw his granddaughter Ganga chatting with boys in the park."

"I was passing through Ravivarpeth and saw Santosh in front of a bar."

"What are you saying? Acharyaru's son drinks?"

"Let it be. Acharyaru is a fine and respected person. What can he do if his children and grandchildren turn out like this? It is their karma."

He awoke at five, drew water from the well and bathed. With chagrin he noted that lights were not turned on in the house. The daughters-in-law did not wake early. They only got up in time to prepare breakfast for their children and ready them for school. His sons also woke up late, bathed, had their breakfast and hurried to the office. No one had the patience to pray even for a few minutes.

With a pang, he remembered his wife. She would be up before him and heat a big glass of milk with almonds and pistachio. Then she swept the courtyard, sprinkled water on the ground in front of the temple, drew intricate patterns of rangoli before the deity, and worshiped the Tulsi plant. Well, that was not happening now.

As he paused in the veranda, he heard a moan as his daughter-in-law made love to her husband. The moan intruded on his morning prayers diverting his mind. However, he consoled himself that they were young and must enjoy carnal pleasure.

He often saw his sons and their wives in intimate positions, and averted his gaze. These people had no shame. They did not dress decently even in front of their children.

He gulped a glass of cold milk in the kitchen and went to his beloved temple, prostrating in front of the idols. He carefully washed the idols, lit incense sticks, and offered flowers.

Then he began his elaborate rituals, and Sandhya-vandanam, the ritual of self-purification, chanting the mantras in Sanskrit.

"Salutations to Lord Achyutha, Anantha and Govinda and the

twelve names of Lord Vishnu, Kesava, Narayana, Madhava, Govinda, Vishnu, Madhusoodhana, Trivikrama, Vamana, Sridhara, HrishikesaPadmanabha, Damodara."

"For the removal of all obstacles I meditate on Lord Vighnesvara who is clad in white, is all-pervading, is white like the moon, sports four arms and is always of serene aspect."

He went through the prescribed steps of the purification Āchamanaand the controlled breathing of Prānāyāma, and the rest to purify his soul and mind. Try as he might, his mind drifted to the lustful moans. Castigating himself, he completed the last step Antya-prakaranani and invoked blessings of the Gods.

Early in the morning, devotees stopped at the temple, bowed to the gods and sipped thirtha, holy water. They lingered for a few minutes, exchanged pleasantries and moved on.

He finished his rituals by noon and went to the house for his lunch. He noticed that the kitchen fire was not lit and there was no sign of cooking. Famished, he broke a coconut, drank the refreshing water and waited.

From the kitchen window he saw a car near the gate and heard voices in the hall. His sons and their wives were discussing something. He leaned forward and heard snatches of the conversation.

"Redevelopment is possible."

"What will we get?"

"Each will get an apartment and money. But you must get signatures on the agreement form."

Acharyaru shuffled in to sudden silence. The guest hurriedly got up, bowed to him and left.

"What is that about? Who is he?"

"Nothing, he is a friend who had come for tea."

"I will get your lunch ready", said Kamala, his third son's wife and hurried out. Others also remembered some work, leaving Acharyaru alone in the room.

Something was going on behind his back. The whispers, furtive glances, and guilty silences were suspicious. Maybe if he kept quiet they would eventually tell him. He prayed, "Oh Deva take care of your temple."

They waited until he finished his food then sat in front of him as he lay on his cot.

"Appa," began Chidananda his eldest son. "My wife Parvati is tired of living here. It leaks, running water is not available, and the place is decrepit."

His second son Gopal nodded, "Even my wife Shanta is depressed with this place. The vast empty space behind the house with overgrown bushes is an eyesore."

"Appa," said his third son Ramesh. "Yesterday, a builder came. He has a fantastic offer."

"Yes, yes", broke in Kamala his third son's wife. "We should take it."

Despair struck him and he felt a tremor run through his chest. The thought of parting with his children and grandchildren left him numb. Old age and loneliness had mellowed him. He looked through tears at his family asked, "You want to leave me and go away?"

"No, no, Appa! It never occurred to us. We will always be with you."

"Then what is this about?"

"See Appa," began Chidananda. "The builder is ready to develop this place. Our old house will go and a new complex will come up."

"Yes Appa," cried Ramesh and Kamala. "We all will get big apartments and five lakh rupees each!"

"What?" shouted the old man, "Tear down the house? What about the temple and the devotees? What about Rayaru? He will be homeless!"

This was unthinkable. They wanted to demolish the temple? He broke into a sweat, felt a sharp pain in his chest and he swooned.

His flustered children sprinkled water on his face and Acharyaru groggily got up. He was sweating profusely and they let him rest. They decided to speak about this later.

Kamala reasoned, "He is old and infirm with none to look after him. We are the only children. What will he do alone in this place? Yes, we will threaten, cry and blackmail him to agree."

Santosh, who was eighteen was brash, cocky, and liked to live a fast life. He wore jeans, tee shirt, listened to pop music, drank alcohol, smoked and imagined himself as a dashing rebel. As per ancient traditions, drinking alcohol and eating meat were sins for Brahmins. Such taboos did not concern Santosh.

That he was Acharyaru's son did not bother him. He did not care about religion nor did he follow the social norms that his family and society expected from him. He was easily recognized and people tended to speak diffidently around him. He got over this problem by wearing a full face helmet on his bike to gain anonymity.

He stole money from the donation box in the temple with a duplicate key. He pilfered just enough now and then to quench his vices and not raise suspicion.

Another of his unacceptable deeds was to fall in love with Sandra. There was nothing wrong with Sandra. She was studying to be a teacher and was assured of a job. However, she was a Christian, and a Brahmin marrying a Christian was unacceptable to the Brahmin community. Santosh was oblivious of the taboo and they moved around on his bike, often eating meat in her house and drinking beer.

"What will become of us Santosh?" she asked one day as they sat under a tree, holding each other.

"Wait until I complete my degree and get a job. We will get married," murmured Santosh.

"When will that happen? My mother is getting very impatient. She wants commitment and an early marriage."

"See Sandra," he said rather boisterously "I am willing to give up my religion and I can decide how to live my life. Tell her that we will get married."

"But Santosh, you steal money from the temple. You have no job, how will you take care of me and the family?"

Santosh fell silent, his arms slipping away from her neck, her presence troubling him. Without the support of his family and community he would not get far. They would ostracize him if he married Sandra.

Sandra represented freedom, a forbidden pleasure, an escape from his strict routine and she appealed to his youthful fervour. She dressed in tee shirts, skirts, and had an open and carefree nature everything that girls from his community did not have.

But, Sandra was also practical and mature. She had been infatuated by his audacious attitude and his good looks and they decided to date. She had never let him go the whole way and had let him fondle her breasts and kiss. After the initial euphoria, the puppy love had evaporated. She wanted marriage and a secure life.

Things came to a climax one day when they sat under their favourite tree in the Karnatak College campus, in the secluded botanical gardens. The trees had heard hundreds of bras unsnapping, seen hundreds of such romances, some successful, many broken.

With a frown she said "Santosh, I have sad news."

"What sad news?"

She moved back, her body tight with resistance, "My mother has found a boy for me. He works at a factory in Hubli. We are getting married."

Stunned, he lurched forward trying to grasp her hand. "Sandra! How can you leave me?"

"Santosh, we have been going around for months. My mother hears gossip about us and she scolds me to get a commitment. Do we have a future? You don't have a job, money, or a house. I need stability and assurance for our future."

They sat silently as she poked at the grass with her foot, grim determination in her eyes. "You are not willing to leave your religion, and your community will not accept me. Let us face the reality."

His face went white with shock and he clasped his head. "But Sandra, I love you."

With finality and a firm voice, she said, "We did have a good time. I did let you touch me, so we are even. This is the last time we meet. Please do not contact me ever. It is over."

Angry and frustrated, Santosh kicked at the favourite tree, bruising himself. He scowled at his friends who waved at him. Sandra always filled his mind and now she was gone leaving a void. He wanted to kill himself, feeling worthless at the rejection. His immaturity blinded him to his inadequacy and inability to provide for her.

Unable to cope, he went to a bar, drank heavily and drove in a drunken stupor. His swollen tear filled eyes did not see the Tempo coming up the road. He crashed into the vehicle and lay bleeding and broken.

Passersby rushed him to the hospital. Dharwad is a small town. They recognized him and they called up his home. Acharyaru and his family ran to the hospital in panic.

The doctor, a devotee of Acharyaru, said, "Acharyaru, the injuries are not serious. He will start walking in a few months."

He motioned Acharyaru and Chidananda aside and spoke to them softly. "Acharyaru, Santosh was drunk. It is a police case now."

Aghast, Acharayru said, "Drunk? Doctor Saheb, there must be some mistake."

"Acharyaru, we smelt alcohol on his breath and as per rules performed a blood test. His blood alcohol level was very high. It is fortunate that he did not hit anyone."

Acharya was in tears, "Doctor Saheb. I don't know what to say.

I brought him up in the strictest tradition."

He stood with folded hands and his head hung low, a picture of abject misery. "What should I do now?"

Acharyaru had never requested or bowed to anyone other than Rayaru. The hurt, shame, and worry for his wayward son were too much.

The doctor held Acharyaru's hands firmly to prevent him from bowing. "Acharyaru, the police inspector and I hold you in great reverence. We will hush up the case."

Acharyaru folded his hands and bowed his head.

News of the accident spread quickly. Friends and disciples of Acharyaru came to the hospital. While Santosh's drunkenness became known, no one blamed Acharyaru. He was a holy man who prayed for all and wished everybody well.

While Santosh recovered, Acharyaru came daily to meet him, his face suffused with pain and misery as he looked at the bandages, feeling the pain of his son.

The old Acharya shuttled between the hospital and his temple on his bicycle. People wondered at his energy and love for the delinquent son.

As the days went by, Santosh listened to footsteps as he lay immobile, waiting for Sandra, who never came.

His friend broke the news to him. "She got married last Sunday. My friend James, her neighbour, attended the wedding."

Well, that thread was now truly broken and he had to move on with his life.

Santosh was remorseful at the shame he had brought to his family and seething with self-revulsion. What a fool he had been. His father was worshipped and here he was in the hospital for drunk driving! He had cheated his father and was not worthy of being his son. What made him take this path of destruction? Did his father know that he drank and ate meat? How could he face Acaharyaru who still loved him?

Acharyaru came every day to the hospital and to pass time, he began to narrate stories from the Mahabharata and the

Bhagavad Gita.

"The gods are outside our bodies waiting to guide us to the path of righteousness. The demons we do not know are inside, leading us on the wrong path. It is up to the individual to decide whom to follow."

The hospital staff and patients stood outside the room and listened to the old man as he struggled to reclaim his lost son. TV, mobile phones, pop songs fell silent as he spoke with a belief and sincerity in simple language that made his sermons appealing and calmed their inner self.

Muslims and Christians listened with reverence. The stories were universal, neither eulogising nor blaming, they transcended religion, caste, god, and appealed to the soul.

After sometime, he began to wait eagerly for his father's visits. He remembered his childhood and the puranas and vedas that his father recited. He longed to hear them again.

Thus began the change gradually from the earlier loathing towards the pious life, to one of thankfulness, and then to reverence.

The discontent at home was boiling over. The daughters-in-law became openly hostile towards Acharyaru. Milk mixed with water was doled out, and sloppily-cooked food was dumped on a plate.

Chidanand spoke out angrily, "What does the old fool think. As heirs, we have equal rights on the property."

Kamala shouted, "Better consult a lawyer and send a court notice."

Ramesh said, "I spoke to a lawyer. We inherit the property only after his death."

"I wonder when he will die," hissed Shanta.

Acharyaru kept silent, bearing the insults and barbs, the snide taunts and to the fights between the sons and their wives. All peace at home was gone and he considered this as his karma, punishment for sins committed unknowingly in the present and the past life.

He reasoned that even Lord Rama and Devi Sita suffered in exile and so did the dharma-bound Pandavas. So who was he to question karma?

Acharyaru pondered deeply into his beliefs and duty. Was he wrong? Was his devotion to the Lord more than the duty to his children? He looked around at the house anew and admitted to himself that it was indeed decrepit. Was it right to deny his children an opportunity to live in a better home? Were they right and was he wrong?

He looked at his clothes and meagre possessions. He had served the Lord for decades and had never become rich. Was it right to force his children to follow his ideals and remain poor?

He picked up the Bhagavad Gita and read a verse, *"Man's fate, wealth, fortune are brought about from his own shrama, hard work. Blaming one's parents and fate for poverty is a folly."*

He accepted that the house was decrepit. Yet he had never stopped his sons from repairing and cleaning the place. They did not study hard and could not get jobs with good pay. So, the fault was not his but their laziness. He decided that he would not sell the temple come what may. Let them do their worst.

The builder was notorious for strong-arm tactics. When a property had multiple owners, some willing owners were bribed, and others threatened to force them to sell. However, threats would not work with Acharyaru for he was respected and hundreds would come to his aid.

Acharyaru's sons gathered in the builder's office greedily fingering the bundle of notes given as an advance. The builder gloated in satisfaction. All the sons except one were 'purchased'. Only the old man and his drunkard son in the hospital remained. The prime property was near a commercial centre, and he would make a killing.

He bid them goodbye and said, "Get the signature of the old man and your brother quickly. Else, my men will come after you."

The sons, their wives and children had a great time. They bought new clothes, sweets, gold and silver, invited their wives' relatives, and spent the entire advance merrily. No one cared for the old man who sat hungry waiting for food that never came.

One Amavasya, the new moon and darkest inauspicious night, they surrounded him.

"So Appa, what have you decided?"

"About what?"

"Are you going to sign the papers or not?"

"Why should I?"

"Muduka," shrieked Kamala, using a crass term for old man. "You have just a few years left to rot. What will you do if we go away?"

Ramesh said, "Tomorrow the builder will come. You better sign the papers."

Acharyaru kept quiet until the tirade ended. "What about the temple? What about Rayaru? Do you think he will forgive you? Do not force me to put a curse on you."

That shut them up. The shouting attracted the neighbours and they came running.

"What! Sell the temple and house? What a shame."

"You sinners! You dare threaten Acharyaru!"

Outnumbered, his sons quickly retreated to their rooms. Usurping the property through threats would not work. They had to find another way.

For the next few days, his sons and daughters-in-law behaved very cordially. They got up at five, offered the Acharya hot milk and bananas, served hot food dripping with ghee, clarified butter and waited on him. They even pressed his aching legs and back.

Acharyaru was not fooled. He knew their wiles and decided to enjoy the good times while they lasted.

Santosh returned home one morning from the hospital, filling Acharyaru with immense joy. He fluttered around the ambulance crew, getting in their way as they carried Santosh into the house. He was placed in a room on the ground floor next to his father's room.

As Acharyaru folded his hands to thank them, the crew prostrated instead thanking God for giving them an opportunity to serve Acharyaru. They refused tips and requested the old man to call in case any help was needed

Santosh hobbled around on his crutches. He sat in front of the temple, greeting devotees, listening to the holy mantras, and reading the scriptures. Acharyaru fussed and catered to all his needs, bathing and feeding him.

His brothers and their wives laughed and taunted him.

"See, that drunk has turned to religion. He will start drinking once he gets well."

"Yes, and this time he will run behind a Muslim girl who will also ditch him."

The builder was getting impatient. He called up the sons and wanted to know when the deal would be done. He sent thugs to hasten the process.

The sons knew that threats would not work with Appa. They tried emotional blackmail instead. One morning, as Acharyaru came out of the temple, he heard shouts.

"I will not stay another instant in this house," shouted Kamala as she stood outside with her children, her clothes tied in a bundle.

"I am going to my father's house in Gadag," screamed Parvati as she dragged her children along.

"Better to live in an anath ashram with other neglected women and children than this naraka hell," screeched Shanta.

They stood outside with their bags and their brood yowling. The old man noticed that there were no tears in their eyes; it was all sound and noise. The three sons approached Acharyaru and fell at his feet.

"Save us Appa. Our wives are leaving."

"So? Let them go."

Chidananda started begging, "Appa, please listen to our prayers. The builder gave us an advance. If you do not sign the papers, they will kill us."

"See Muduka," shrilled Shanta. "You will die very soon. We will then sell this house. So why don't you give it up now."

Parvati shouted, "Who will perform the rituals when you lie on your deathbed? Santosh? Your drunkard son?"

Santosh was not to be seen, a fact that did not escape their notice.

Acharyaru walked down the steps to the courtyard, "It is better to nurture a snake than you people. You have no respect for god, traditions and elders. Shameless people, go away from here."

His voice trembled with anger. "You know the meaning of a Brahmin? We are the mediators between Gods and the devotees. When devotees bow and ask for my blessings, they pray to the god who is embodied in me."

He looked at Kamala, "I am no god, but an Acharya, the conscience of my devotees. The temple that you want to sell gives people courage to face difficulties. When they pray, their soul is filled with strength and belief. They face their problems bravely and accept what God gives them, good or bad. The temple stands for faith."

They listened in agitated silence as he continued, "For a hundred years, my ancestors served our people, giving them hope and faith. Without faith one is nothing."

His sons and their wives watched him with rising panic. Shanta shouted, "Enough of this nonsense. Why don't you sign the papers, else, we will go."

"Leave if you want to," he said, "As for your debts, settle them by selling your gold."

Kamala cried, "You are old. Who will care for you? When you die what will become of this temple?"

"When I die? Yes, death is inevitable. We will see about that when my final day comes. I am sure Rayaru will answer my prayers."

Parvati yelled, "Who is left, Muduka? Your drunkard son? He will marry a Muslim and this temple will become a Masjid."

"Stop!" A voice rang out, silencing the group.

Santosh stumbled and came forward. "You forget that Appa has another son. I will continue the pooja and rituals. The temple will remain until Rayaru wills it otherwise."

Santosh stood with his crutches, clad in a crisp white Dhoti and the angavastaram, the top cloth of a Brahmin. The sacred thread, the Janawara dropped softly from his left shoulder. Streaks of fresh sandal paste glinted on his forehead and arms.

"Ha, look at this drunkard, now he wants to be an Acharya," the group laughed derisively.

"Yes, I have sinned and repented. The long hours in the hospital and Appa's love made me realise my mistake. I regained my faith, something that you never had. If Appa is ready to accept me, I will serve in the temple as his servant until he deems me fit for full service."

Tears fell from Acharyaru's eyes as he hugged his son.

"Appa, I am a sinner," confessed Santosh. "I drank alcohol, ate meat, and stole money."

"Yes, my dear son. I knew that. I kept quiet, waiting for your sins to boil over and cleanse your soul. The life of an Acharya is very tough. You have to fight your own demons and insecurities to inspire people to keep their faith. You have to ask your inner voice if you really repent."

"Yes Appa I repent. The past has shown me my mistakes and the true path. If you and Rayaru accept me, I will become your disciple. I will learn the scriptures and the rituals. I know it will take time, but I am ready."

"Then rise, my son. Step into the temple and ask Rayaru for mercy and forgiveness. I pray that the Gods accepts you."

The other sons and their wives stood gaping and glowered at the two in frustrated anger unable to comprehend the changed situation. Their dreams of wealth evaporated. This drunkard Santosh who was the butt of their sarcastic jokes was now the saviour while they had become the villains.

At peace, Acharayaru looked back at them and said, "A repentant sinner is better than a faithless one."

REDEMPTION, REFORMATTED

BY
LELA MARKHAM

Beyond Rock Bottom
by Ryan Seymour
I quit drinking because the bottle's empty,
so it's best not to restart.
It's like I thought life's answers
were at the bottom of that bottle,
but when I got there,
I forgot all the questions.

That's what I learned during my latest stint in court-ordered rehab. Brilliant, huh? Four weeks of talking about my *feelings* and that's what I came up with. To my credit, I spent the first week puking and shaking, so not much stuck in my head. On the third day, I paused puking long enough to admit I'd lost control of my life and most especially, drinking. Then came Step 2.

I've kicked that troll in less pleasant places–jail and under a bush in the park where I live–maybe a dozen times. I always picked up the bottle as soon as I scraped together any money, sometimes buying alcohol instead of food. Drinking had been my more-or-less full-time occupation for two years, interfering with paying jobs and making rent. But all that changed six months ago.

On my fourth time in rehab I didn't duck on Step 2. I actually thought about it. Alcoholics *need* a higher power. I clearly needed something *deeper* than AA, a spiritual journey that was an encounter with God as I understood it/him/her/whatever and when I meditated on this on the fourth day, a verse from a long-forgotten Sunday School lesson crawled out of the detoxifying fog.

"God is close to the brokenhearted." Not "God will let me near Him if I go looking for Him when I'm sober" but He's already here beside me in the toxic mud right now. Which meant I could talk to Him and, if I shut up my self-centered whine fest for longer than half a moment, He could talk to me. I grew up in church, but I'd somehow missed that lesson until I was hanging my head over a toilet for several days. For the fourth time.

They're Big Book thumpers in rehab, but when one of the counselors brought me a Bible, I dug through it until I found it. Psalm 34:18. It was the first time I'd ever made an actual effort to get sober and I made it all the way to Step 5 in rehab. That's at least one step further than most relapsed AAs ever make it, and I'm staring Step 9 straight in its terrifying eye now. I am an overachiever when I have a goal.

In Step 9 you offer to make amends to the people you screwed over, and I've got nothing. My gas tank is empty. I know I owe them, but how in the world am I going to pay anything back in my present state? I shouldn't be here. I graduated with a degree coveted by IT professionals that I stole money from my dad to get. Yeah, I slouched this way for years, but I'm not some waste-case without skills to get out of this mess. It's just I can't apply for a decent job when I'm living under a bush with no computer access or means to keep myself clean. Without a steady job, I can't get off the streets. Yeah, that lizard is chasing its tail and I couldn't pay back a quarter, let alone what I owe my dad.

I wake up under my bush, shivering, hungry, and 189 days sober. The first three are a normal morning when you're homeless. This hard-scrabble park is filled with people who aren't going anywhere because there is nowhere left for us to go. Just to be clear, I have no one to blame but me for being in this condition.

Today is one of those days when I wish that weren't true, but I know it is.

It's a gray day suggesting rain or snow and the day labor agent doesn't choose me, so I sit on a park bench scratching filthy fingers through greasy hair while contemplating the joys of day drinking–if I only had the money and–oh, yeah–hadn't quit. Being sober doesn't mean you don't still want it and there are days, when I'm cold, hungry, tired, and fed up, I want it more than others. My buddy Luke and I agree I'd have other excuses if I had a job, roof, and food to eat, so the circumstances of my life are not a reason to drink. That's why I get up off my butt to ask Ilene, the owner of a nearby coffee shop, if I can clean the windows for some food. Today I prefer food over money because once I have food in my system, I'll remember that I can't get out of this cesspit if I go back to drinking.

I do a great job on the windows because it's warm in the coffee shop and I'm so tired of being cold. A bone-deep ache seeps into my soul so far, I fear I'll never be warm again. Ever since rediscovering my Higher Power in rehab, I've been praying every day almost all day and Jesus has helped me to stay sober and figure out where I've gotten life wrong, but as the days get shorter and the nights colder, I've been praying for rescue. I know– selfish. God is not my cosmic Sugar Daddy. I know I made this mess I'm dying in. I'm also certain that if He doesn't intervene on my behalf soon, I'm going to end up a statistic under that bush.

The handymen on my dad's ranch, lowliest of hands, have food to eat, a warm bed, and they get to take a shower every night. I used to look down on their uneducated, menial-labor existences but now I'd rejoice to be them. If I could afford a bus ticket home, I'd beg Dad to let me work for room and board until I paid off my debt. When I blew out of his house six years ago, I thought I wanted freedom, but I only found the slavery of bad choices and crushing shame. I want my freedom of choices back. I'm fighting tears while washing windows when all of the sudden, I hear my name.

"Ryan?"

I freeze before turning my head. The guy's a normal, dressed in pressed jeans and a slouchy, casual coat that cost more than I've made in the last year. There's a beanie atop his expensive haircut, a five-dollar cup of coffee in one hand and a leather computer bag over his shoulder. I don't recognize him, which makes me intensely nervous.

"Al. We were on the same floor at UW." It's only been two years and a few months since graduation, but a lot of crap has happened to me since then, so it takes a second to remember him. He holds out a hand to shake. We weren't friends. He was a preacher's kid from another ranch community and I remember him as a bigger Bible-thumper than my brother Zach, which even now isn't really a good thing in my book.

"Hi," I say, not reaching for his hand. "You were in Hutchinson's coding class and you have no idea where my hands have been."

"Right." He pauses as if stumped for what to say next. Yeah, you chose to kick a hornet's nest, pal. I'm not angry that you're standing there enjoying the benefits of the career I blew off to chase my addiction, but you've just realized that I might be. Go on. Remember an urgent appointment. "Can I buy you something to eat, man?" he asks instead.

"They pay me in food for doing this," gesturing broadly to the large café windows. I immediately regret my over-sharing because getting cash today might not be a good thing. His eyes twitter, and Ilene, the shop owner, speaks up from the cash register.

"You can come collect your payment in the morning." Ilene is always kind to me. Even before I got sober, I wasn't belligerent with her, although there are other places where I'm not welcome because of my past behavior.

"I just want to talk with you," Al explains. "But you look like you could use a meal."

Ilene's eyes beg me to be sensible, so I say "yes" and we take a booth. I gotta figure I stink, but he ignores it and says I can order anything I want.

"How are you doing?" I ask instead because I'm not used to getting anything I want and what I really want today is not on Ilene's menu. I want it, I don't need it. What I *need* is food. A warm bed. A shower. One out of three ain't bad.

"Good. I work for Bunnell & Wilson."

Ouch! I blew off a guaranteed job at B&W by going on a two-month bender, spending the last of my ill-gotten college fund, and ending up in jail on a DUI charge. Life went downhill from there.

"Good for you." I admire anyone who can make a sensible choice without four trips to rehab. He examines my face.

"How long have you been sober?"

Most people just see a homeless addict, maybe someone who paused drinking for the day.

"How do you know I am?"

"Your eyes. You've clearly been living rough, but it's the first time I've ever seen you without that glassy look." I'm not surprised that some people knew back in college. My first trip to rehab was in 11th grade, so I know I wasn't a mystery to the observant.

"Six months."

"And you're homeless?" I nod, so used to the shame I no longer try to lie about it. "Why?"

Honesty is a humiliating sobriety tool at times. I embrace it.

"I'm stuck." There's no judgment in his eyes. "I can't get a job like this and I need a job to not be like this. I work at what I can—this, day labor—but I never make enough consistently enough to get off the streets." I stop myself before whining about circumstances beyond my control.

"You rack up a record?"

"DUI, vagrancy, resisting arrest, some drunk and disorderly. No felonies." I'm not really proud of that last bit. I've been lucky to not slide that far over the cliff, which would disqualify me from a lot of jobs. I can see he's doing mental calculus.

"Order some food and eat and then I'm going to ask you to earn it. You okay with that?"

"With earning it. Not a problem. With imposing upon your generosity, yeah. You order what you're willing to pay for. I'm going to go wash my hands."

Ilene lets me use the bathroom to clean up since I will leave it better than I found it. Yeah, not all of us are jerks; just enough that shop owners lock their bathrooms. There's a sandwich and a bowl of soup waiting when I come back to the table. Forget about polite when I sit down. I almost make myself sick, I eat so fast and way beyond my stomach capacity. It's been four days. I can't help myself. Al waits until I set aside the half of the sandwich I can't eat. Luke will be thankful for some food.

As I sip the warm coffee, I'm a little panicked because I don't really know Al and I'm *not* paying for the meal with my body, so things could turn really bad any minute. That last drunk and disorderly, the one that sent me to rehab, was me saying "no" to someone people don't think of as a bad man. It would have been an assault charge if my public defender hadn't told the guy I would blab about him in open court. I don't regret it, even though I'm banned from the Rescue Mission for a year. That was my rock bottom, which is good, though it means I'm going to spend the winter under a bush … if I make it that far.

Al pulls out his laptop. Some guys like me would grab it and run, but I know you can't hock a double-encrypted high-end Dell and I've given up being a thief since my one and only foray into that crime made me feel like crap. Al types something then turns the screen to me. I haven't touched a computer in two years, so that I recognize it as a coding challenge is a good sign.

"Can you solve it?" He tries to read my expression.

"It's been a while. I can try."

"I'm going to read a book while you do it. Just take your time and if you blow it once or twice, start over. You want some more coffee?"

I stare at the screen, scared, but I nod, then grunt "Decaf" because my hands are already shaking. Ilene responds, he pulls out a paperback, and I focus. An hour later, I've crashed once, then cleared five levels, none of them in record time, but with a fair degree of accuracy. I'm way rusty at coding, but I haven't forgotten. I momentarily relish the feeling of accomplishment. He looks up when I sigh, turning the screen to him to scan the results.

"You know I got your job?"

"I knew someone did." I shrug. We both know I screwed up. Jealousy won't fix that.

"Would a job solve your problems?"

My heart speeds up as I feel a long-closed gate to better times crack open, then my life lessons slam on my brakes. I'm in this mess for a reason. I'm the rich young ruler seeking the kingdom of God, blocked at the narrow gate by my baggage.

"It would help, but–." I'm terrified to trust a stranger to understand my failures, hoping his faith isn't as shallow as I once thought he was, risking whatever opportunity he's offering. I'm starving and used up and how I live *matters*. "I'd probably just back myself into relapse if it was too easy."

"Easy? You're living on the streets, man. There's nothing been easy with your life for a while."

"It was too easy before. I thought my talent was a golden ticket. I hurt my family, my dad, and when what I thought I wanted was within my reach, I chose to self-destruct because I knew I didn't deserve it. I understand it. Now. I think I've learned my lesson, but I also know I can't just take a job and move forward. I have to meet my obligations to my dad before I can be truly free. I don't know if there's a way to work that out."

"With God, all things are possible," Al says. I theoretically believe that, but there's been no practical application of that concept in my life. A stupid AA aphorism pops into my head–*Let go and let God*. "What do you need? Maybe I can help."

He buys me a bus ticket to my home town of Antioch, a ranch town northwest of Olympia. I've got two weeks to claim the job and Al will help me with housing to get started. Or if my dad doesn't throw me out on my ear, I can telecommute. Maybe it'll work out. That's not been the course of my life in recent years, so I'm scared as I leave the bus station.

Ranch communities are spread out, and when I was a kid, I really hated that we lived so far from town. Now, still dressed in my grubby clothes and exhausted from not sleeping, I'm kind of glad the road is long. I'm terrified of what happens at my destination, so I keep rehearsing my speech as I walk. I really expect to be rejected, but whatever happens, I know it's the right thing to come here before I start the next stage of my life. I haven't felt less like drinking since ... ever.

A truck passes going the other direction. I'm not hitchhiking because I doubt anyone will pick me up, but then that same truck pulls up in front of me and brakes hard. I stop walking, wary. I got mugged this way several months ago. Unless I put up my thumb, don't stop for me. The driver's door pops open and I prepare to run in the opposite direction, but then I stare at my dad as he stares at me.

"I'm sorry," I blurt as he closes the distance between us. I flinch. He's never hit me, but plenty of other people have since I left his house. He draws me in instead, babbling about Mrs. Ainsley. I stand in his hug, tears spilling down my face, stiff as a board, terrified to move and super self-conscious about the way I must smell. This is *not* the way I pictured this going.

"You're here," he observes, holding my head in his hands, staring as if my face is a treasure he's been seeking for a lifetime. He's crying too, but I'm scared he'll remember he's angry with me. There's things I need to say before it's too late. "Let's get you home." He turns toward the truck, but I drag my feet. He grabs my backpack strap like I'm a skittish horse. "It's fine, son."

"It's not," I croak. "I stole from you."

"It can all be worked out. Get in the truck and come home."

He steers me to the passenger door and I don't resist because snot is running into my whiskers and I just want to say how sorry

I am. I start again as he puts the truck in gear.

"I stole from you and I haven't got the money to pay you back, but I'm willing to work it off if you'll let me." I repeat myself while he turns into the long driveway. When he parks the truck, I stare at the house, shivering.

"Welcome home, son."

It's not and can't be, so long as the theft stands between us, but I let him steer me into the house. He takes me right up to my old room and opens the bathroom door, suggesting a shower and shave while he makes dinner.

"You don't have to," I whisper. I have eaten today, but a shower would be nirvana. I'd pictured him grudgingly letting me stay in the bunkhouse, not acting like I've just come home from college. I never came home from college because I expected to be ushered to a jail cell.

"I want to."

By the time he comes back with a razor and shaving cream, I've managed to peel down to my thread-bare briefs. I think my clothes and body probably stink worse now that I've disturbed the bubble. His gaze takes in the ravages of my life since I left school. Every rib shows and my collar bones could cut cheese.

He tells me I can take as long as I need, so I do. I make use of the nail clippers and scissors that are in the medicine cabinet because I haven't seen a barber shop in a long time. Even with warm water and a lot of soap, it takes a long time sitting in the tub to get all the grime out of my skin. Then I scrub my filth from the tub and take another shower. I'm actually hungry now. When I come out, my bag is gone. I panic for a second because being stolen from on the street can be the precipitating spiraling event, but there's a neat stack of ranch-casual clothes on the bed. I've gotten taller and lost a lot of weight since leaving home, so I have to dig in the closet for a belt to keep the jeans up. There's no shoes and he's taken my worn-out boots, but I find socks in the drawer so I'm at least not spreading whatever is growing on my feet all over his floors.

"Those boots had holes," he says when I come into the kitchen. "Have to get you some new ones."

"Not your responsibility," I remind him. "What did you do with my stuff?"

"I'm washing it, but it's mostly falling apart, so you may not get it back. What happened to you out there?"

Honesty is hard, but it's all I've got to offer.

"*I* happened to me out there. A lot of bad decisions, starting before I stole your money."

"You started drinking again." He knows me, who I used to be.

"I never really stopped."

I hid my increasing addiction the last sixteen months at home so well he trusted me to handle a bull sale where I had access to a lot of cash. I had a great plan for his money and I did accomplish it before flushing it all down the toilet.

"I found several bottles hidden in your room after you left for school."

I don't want to rehash my past. I'm not that person anymore.

"Six months sober," I tell him. "It's not a huge accomplishment, but it's the longest I've made it since high school."

"Then I'm proud of you."

"I'm a thief, Dad. What's to be proud of?"

"Are you still a thief?"

I haven't stolen anything since I took Dad's money. I had lots of reasons to steal the last couple of years, but even at my worst, I knew I didn't want to feel guilty about anything else.

"I think I'm still a thief until I pay you back."

"We'll talk about that, but you need to eat and rest. You been sick?"

"Not really." Out of shape and underweight, but 23-year-olds can bounce back, the rehab staff said. "Just living rough. Kind of got stuck and couldn't figure a way out. I was hoping...." I pause because it's hard to beg and he takes me by the shoulders.

"We will talk about this *tomorrow*."

I'd forgotten what a good cook my father is. He's done a dish with white fish and lemons with rice pilaf and a salad. After two bites, I mist up. He pats my arm.

"Eat. Get a good night's sleep. We'll deal with this tomorrow when you're not so tired."

As soon as I eat, I'm yawning. I can't eat much anyway, and he's not angry that I can't show my appreciation by eating more. He's worried by it. I go off to bed right after I admit I'm stuffed, and I sleep deeply, though I wake up in the dark of the night sweating then shivering. I smell breakfast as my alarm, my stomach growling before I even open my eyes. My battered Bible sits on the nightstand, though everything else from my pack is still missing and he still hasn't given me any shoes. I rub some of the extra-strength cream he's supplied into my foot fungus then flip my Bible to Romans 5, all about hope stemming from standing in the grace of God through faith in Christ. So where I'm living this morning! Grace is a difficult concept. I can't earn it. I can only accept it by faith and trust that God will use it to my good. Not even two days ago, I admitted I couldn't fix my life on my own and hoped for rescue while Al was ordering coffee. Now I'm sitting in my high school bedroom, freshly showered, having slept in a warm bed, and wearing clean clothes. Amazing grace that saved a screw-up like me!

Dad wrinkles his nose when I come into the kitchen.

"Those are the same clothes you wore yesterday."

"For an hour," I remind him. The kitchen is awash with morning sun. "I meant to be up earlier than this." Waking at dawn under the bush had been easier when in touch with the sky, but warmth more than made up for that loss.

"I turned off your alarm when I brought you the Bible. I wanted you to wake up to the smell of bacon and know that you are home."

I sigh, burdened with shame. It's worse that he's not angry. Did I need him to be angry, so I'd have an excuse to self-destruct? I hope not.

"So can we talk about it now or-."

"After breakfast. Eat."

I don't turn down free meals these days. He doesn't put so much on my plate but leaves seconds if I want it. I haven't finished eating when Joe McAllister comes to the door and congratulates me on coming home. The ranch foreman, he announces there'll be grilled burgers at noon to celebrate my return. I bite my tongue until he leaves.

"Dad, I don't want to celebrate coming home," I say as soon as Joe closes the door. "I can't pretend when I owe you."

He gives me a gentle smile, refilling my coffee mug without asking.

"Your debt's got nothing to do with me being happy you're home. I tried to find you soon as I calmed down. That took a couple of months. I sent your brother to the university to track you down, but he said you weren't there."

Zach lied, but that's not really who I know him to be, so maybe I'm misremembering. What I *remember* is he yelled at me for taking the money and told me Dad would press charges. I'd probably been drinking, so I'd yelled back. It's between me and Zach so I don't say any of this to Dad.

"When I saw your name on the graduation list, I went myself, but you'd disappeared."

My cheeks burn with shame and here I am freshly shaved so I can't hide it in my beard.

"I planned to pay you back when I got a job. Bunnell & Wilson offered me a good one, but–." I sigh and I'm surprised he lets me continue. "You're going to think I lost my mind because I did–as soon as I got my degree I blew off the job offer and went on a months-long tear. The last couple of years are blurry, but they were really stupid, and I regret most of the choices I made."

"Stolen bread tastes sweet until it poisons you." Yeah! He knows me. "Why'd you steal it? All you had to do was stay sober and I'd have given you the money."

"I know. Now. I wasn't ready to hear it then. All I heard you saying was that I had to earn it when I figured I had already done that. It was a mind-trip I played on myself that had nothing to do with you. I thought I'd be *free*. I enslaved myself to my sin of choice and then deluded myself into thinking degradation was freedom."

"You came to your senses eventually."

"I was forced, but I've stayed sober since by doing what I need to do, including making amends with you."

"You came home. That's enough for me to forgive you."

Yeah, get behind me, Satan!

"But it's not enough for me to feel forgiven and that guilt's going to eat me alive if I don't at least try to make amends."

We're clearing the table and he pauses at the counter like he expects something of me, but I've honestly forgotten how to load a dishwasher. I stare at it anxiously before he hands me a plate and I rinse it before handing it back to him to put in the dishwasher. I watch what he does. I so would have gotten it wrong. It might take some time to relearn indoor living.

"So what are you willing to do?" he asks. I go with my first offer.

"Let me be a ranch hand, work for room and board."

He frowns and gives me this odd smile.

"That'll take twenty years to pay off that debt. I am not a slave-owner, son. If that's what you're offering, the year of Jubilee starts today."

Is he checking to see how well I know my Bible? Hebrews only held slaves for seven years and the year of Jubilee meant the bond was discharged, even if the full debt was still unpaid. I know in my heart my obligation would never *feel* discharged. I laugh because I'm feeling more confident. I didn't come empty-handed.

"I appreciate that but staying here will put a roof over my head while I give you my paychecks. A friend offered me a telecommuting job. Entry level, so it'll take about two years to pay off the principle. I'm hoping you'll take my ranch wages as rent."

I may need a refresher on the dishwasher, but I did scrub pots and pans for the soup kitchen a while back, so I clean the griddle and frying pans while he mulls that over, wiping down the table.

"Are you strong enough for ranch work?" he finally asks.

I sigh. He's seen me virtually naked, so it's a fair question.

"I'm probably going to struggle at first, but if I eat regularly and build up to it, yeah."

He looks sad. I'm starting to panic, afraid he'll reject me, or worse, be too easy on me.

"You worried I'm just going to steal from you again and run off down the road once I'm healthy?"

"Hmm. I'm sorry I think that when you're asking for a chance to prove you've changed."

"What do I need to do to convince you to give me that chance?"

"I'll give you the chance, Ryan. You're the one who has to live with my doubts for however long it takes for this fist in my gut to relax."

"Thieves probably should expect to be doubted until they've repaid what they stole." Draining the sink, I take my time wiping down the countertop before asking for what I need. "Don't give me access to cash or bank cards that don't belong to me. I've absolutely earned that. But, I do need you to trust me a little bit."

"With what?"

"Shoes." He blinks at me a couple of times and then cracks a grin. "You're trying to cut me off at the pass, but really, I got most of the way here under my own power, so you just need to trust me that I'm not going to run away again. 'Cuz I'm going to need shoes to work on the ranch."

Nodding, he claps me on the shoulder.

"I snagged some tennis shoes from your closet while you were cleaning up and I've got an old pair of work boots you can use out on the ranch. But before we get started...." He pauses, and I try not to panic. "I want to know about the Bible."

Yeah, I guess I'd want to know that too if I were him.

"When I hit rock bottom, I met Jesus in the pit. Well, met Him again and listened to Him this time. Talking to Him every day is how I stay sober. One way, anyway."

"There's a meeting a couple of times a week at the church."

"For alcoholics?" He nods. "Good to know. My old bike around here somewhere?" He starts to open his mouth but I get there first. "I lost my license, Dad, so don't offer me car keys."

"I was going to offer to drive you. You haven't earned that level of trust yet."

Since we're establishing ground rules....

"Good for you. Good for me, actually. Things shouldn't be easy for me. I don't do well with easy."

"Yeah, well, you're going to have to put up with easy through today. I want to celebrate that you're back before I start making you earn it."

"I should probably call Al—my job offer—before I go any further. Can I use your phone for a long-distance call?"

"Of course." He pulls his cell phone out of his pocket and holds it out toward me. It's another luxury I don't want to be tempted with while I owe so much.

"I meant the home phone, Dad." I've worried him again, but he accepts it.

"You know where it is."

Al wasn't shining me on. The job offer is still open. He'll drive out next weekend to bring out the equipment I'll need to work. It's barely mid-morning and my brain hurts from all the changes. I ask Dad for a half hour, so I can read the Bible and take care of myself before he shows me around the ranch. He assures me it's fine, that I need to be honest about what I need to stay healthy. Forty-five minutes later, I put on those tennis shoes.

Dad and Zach have expanded the ranch in my absence. We're checking out the new sheep pens when I ask the question burning a hole in my gut.

"Where's Zach?"

"Auction in Centralia." I try not to squirm at memories of my screw-up. "He should be home by midafternoon."

I knew there'd be worse hurdles than Dad. At least I have a couple of hours before I face the beloved older brother. I remember a lot of the ranch hands. They seem to be mostly happy to see me, though I know some of them wonder how long it will take me to have a meltdown. I'm in remission. I haven't gone on a drunken rant in 191 days, although I did dissolve into a bawling mess a few times in the early days of rehab.

Dad doesn't drink, never really has, but he doesn't dictate to the hands on the subject, so there's beer on ice at the barbecue. There's soda too and I sip a too sweet Coke while the burgers finish. I don't want to freak Dad out, so I turn so I can't look at the beer cooler. Just because I want it doesn't mean I'm going to drink it, but he doesn't know that, and I'm trying to be sensitive to our history.

I'm just biting into a fat juicy burger when everybody facing me stops talking. I set the burger down because I know I'm about to lose my appetite. Zach has that effect on me. Always has. I hope he won't always make me insane, but I doubt it will be today.

He's the golden child, light to my dark. While I was smart enough that even heavy drinking didn't dim my intellectual bulb much, Zach was compliant, respectful, and predictable. Not dumb, just not flashy about it. He *never* blew off curfew, he *liked* going to church, and he *wanted* to stay on the ranch to raise cattle, horses, and crops. I could never live up to his stellar example.

"Dad, can we talk?" Zach asks in a flat tone. He's not going to make a public spectacle because that's not what good and healthy people do, but he's pissed. I can feel the undertone. I try and fail to meet his gaze. I should be angry that he lied to me when he found me at UW. I might have made different choices if I hadn't thought Dad would have me arrested if I came home. Or not. The "what if" game involves a road not traveled and I only know what I did. I'm not angry because I have a lot to atone for, even with Zach.

"Have a burger," Dad encourages. "We can talk later."

Zach's jaw tightens. He looks like our mom, lighter with sky blue eyes. I got Dad's dark hair with eyes like new denim. For so long, we seemed to have swapped the souls of the parent we resemble, but I'm not like her. I've just been hurt by her. Someday I'll need to deal with that, but I've got enough to face right here and right now.

"Why are we celebrating?" Zach demands. That would hurt if I hadn't anticipated his anger.

"Don't do this, Zach," Dad cajoles. "We're celebrating your brother's return."

Joe McAllister claps me on the shoulder, so I glance at him. He indicates I should eat my burger. I don't see Zach leave, but I do see Dad follow him. I want to go with them, but I've not been invited, so I try to pretend I still want to eat a burger. I've eaten throwaways from dumpsters, so my gag reflex is well controlled but swallowing that delicious bit of beef, pickle, and bun takes effort. Joe winces, watching me swallow.

"Don't worry," he says. "Zach's a judgmental stone-chucker, but your dad gets it. He wants you here. Long as you're trying, he'll let you stay." He pulls a key ring out of his pocket and holds it so I can see the double XX on the metal tag. He's walked the path I'm currently on. "Pat's a good man and his heart was breaking while you were gone running wild and free."

I laugh nervously.

"Yeah, wild, but far from free. Turns out complete freedom without rules, not even keeping promises to myself, ends up starving on the streets." Joe nods. If he's been in AA for 20 years, he probably has some idea how bad it got. "I thought I would die out there until God gave me another chance. So my freedom in Christ is voluntarily trying to make things right here."

"Your dad said you got a job." Of course, he knows about my stealing the bull money. As foreman, he sees the books. And, yet there's been no judgment from him. I tell him about Al and Bunnell & Wilson.

"So you could have stayed in Seattle and just sent money?" I nod. "Coming here gives you a chance to show them–both of them–you've changed, and you get to be in a safe place while you rebuild your life. Just remember–you can't fix Zach. He'll come around or he won't, and you can't let that color your relationship with your dad. Pat loves you. That never changed, and it won't change, even if you screw up again. He's already forgiven you."

I'm uncomfortable with that and here's a sober Christian who might be able to explain why.

"I haven't earned that."

"And you don't need to. That's the thing about loving parents–we love because of who we are, not because of what our kids do. That's a lesson I had to learn, and Pat's the one who taught it to me. So, sure, meet your obligation so you can be free of the guilt, but it's not going to change how he feels about you."

I decide to ask for some older, wiser counsel.

"Should I go talk to them?"

"You weren't invited. The conversation right now is not between you and Zach. I bet I know what Pat's saying to him though." I question with my expression. "He's been in the bosom of family all this time while you were lost and wandering in the wilderness. Pat's got a right to celebrate you coming home and your brother really doesn't have anything to say about it. But, Ryan." I feel the admonition coming, so I look him right in the eye. "Grace is a gift with a value greater than emeralds, but guys like us will use anything as an excuse for complacency, so just remember–while Pat and Zach are your creditors, you owe yourself and your Savior so much more than you owe them. Regardless of how things work out with your family, you need to stay sober for *you*, because drinking gets in the way of your relationship with Jesus as much or more than it does with your relationship with your folks. And, if you need someone to help you keep your head straight, I'm just down the lane, right?"

"Yes. Thank you. I was sober out there for six months, and one thing I learned from doing that is that the circumstances of my life don't dictate whether I drink. They're not an excuse for me to sin. So, yeah, I'll show up at your door. There's meetings in town, I hear."

I haven't even eaten half my burger, but I'm full because...

starvation diet. I'm helping to clean up the patio as a chill wind blasts out of the north, reminding me that I'm not going to die of hyperthermia tonight. Zach clears his throat and says my name. I turn to look at him, but I still can't meet his gaze. I'm *not* going to die of shame, but it sure feels like it.

"Welcome home," he says in a grudging tone.

Zach is perfect, and I am so not, but Joe claps my shoulder and says he'll be headed to town around 7:30 and I nod and say I'll go with him. Then I turn back to Zach.

"Give me a chance. I'll try not to screw up again."

"And I'm supposed to believe that?"

I know he won't, not yet.

"I got lost, Zach, but I'm back on the right path now. I get I'm hard to trust and there's no one to blame for that but me. You don't have to believe that I've changed. I just hope–If you'd just give me a chance to show you that I've changed. 'Cuz I just–I just really need another chance. And, I think I'm ready for it this time."

I take my leave of Zach and head toward the house where I know my father is waiting and I smile, because I won't be turned away there. Grace is more than enough to give me the one more chance I need.

ALLEGIANCE OWED
BY
JOSEPH W. KNOWLES

Pyotr Simonov read the words for what must have been the hundredth time that night. The *right* to profess religion and to conduct religious worship; it was right there in black and white. Despite his persistence, the words still felt as hollow as ever. He crumpled his page of sermon notes on which he had written these lines from his country's constitution. He tossed it into the waste paper basket at the end of the last small pew of the empty church.

Hours ago, his wife and children had been the last ones to leave, while Pyotr had remained to pray. He was doing this for them, he reassured himself. No loyalty, save one, mattered more in this world. He knew that what he was asking his family and his congregation to do now could put all of them in danger. Even raising the topic had become dangerous since the Council for Religious Affairs had begun increasing their actions against unregistered or uncooperative churches in his town of Ulyanovka.

Turning off the hallway light, Pyotr cinched the laces on his boots as tight as they would go before securing his scarf. It would be a long walk back to his family's apartment and the streets were quickly filling with snow on this mid-January night.

Reaching into his pockets to check for his key, his hand closed around the small bishop chess piece that he had confiscated from his son Yegveny just after the meeting had started. Thinking back, Pyotr decided that he had been too harsh. The boy's active mind sometimes made it difficult for him to sit still and such an insignificant trinket would not have been a serious cause for distraction. This was all somewhat new to the boy, after all.

A sudden gust sliced at his exposed cheeks as he stepped outside, and a flake of snow momentarily blinded him. Blinking, he looked up to see the familiar figure waiting under the light across the narrow street. Pyotr judged it better to meet him head on.

"Good evening, Yuri. I'd best get home before much more of this snow piles up." He had always tried to be cheerful when speaking with Yuri, but it never seemed to have any noticeable effect.

"Moscow will hear about this, you know," the other man sneered. "I don't have to tell you what that could mean for you." He leaned closer, tapping a finger on Pyotr's chest. "And your family."

Pyotr stroked his chin calculatingly and realized from the stubble on his face just how long a day it had been. Now Yuri seemed determined to make it just a little bit longer. But that didn't mean he had to rise to the provocation. The two men had completed their secondary education at the same time, but their paths had diverged sharply from there. Even in his youth, Yuri had been one to hold a grudge and throw his weight around. Pyotr pondered whether, perhaps, that was what suited Yuri so well to his job with the CRA. Just as quickly as the thought entered his mind, he set it aside.

Looking down at the finger still planted in his chest he simply said, "Yes, Yuri," and nodded.

Seeming to be satisfied that Pyotr was sufficiently intimidated, the apparatchik scoffed, shook his head, and turned to go his own way.

Pyotr closed his eyes again briefly. "Lord, forgive him and protect my flock from such men and their bureaucracies," he prayed silently.

Arriving at the apartment, he found his wife, Sofia, still awake, sitting by the stove that heated their small quarters. Peeking behind the curtain that separated them from the apartment's other room, he saw three angelic faces sleeping the peaceful sleep of children who would not understand.

"Elena will be the least able to bear it," his wife said flatly.

At only seven years old, the truth of his wife's statement weighed heavily on him. Josef, of course, was not really a child any more, but Pyotr still found it difficult to think of him as the young man he was quickly becoming. Yegveny–his quick-witted Zhenya–would turn ten next week. Would that God would allow him to be home to celebrate in their small way.

Pyotr hung up his scarf and kissed his wife gently on the forehead.

"Trust in God, my dearest," he whispered as he embraced her. He felt her suppress a sob. Then as she looked up, tears streaming down her face, she whispered back, "What? Shall we receive good at the hand of God, and shall we not receive evil?"

Hearing his beloved wife repeat the words of faithful Job was too much for Pyotr. He sank to his knees, laid his head on his wife's lap, and wept.

Morning dawned cold and clear. Pyotr knew that the snow had stopped just before daybreak because sleep had utterly evaded him. He passed the time praying for his family and every member of his congregation by name. Then he prayed for Yuri.

When Sofia woke and stepped out of the bedroom, Pyotr shuffled in as quietly as he could. He took the contraband bishop from his pocket and laid it on the pillow next to Zhenya's outstretched hand.

Nothing happened that day or the next, but that did not make passing the time any easier. On Saturday evening, just after the children were in bed, Pyotr took the family Bible out of its hidden nook and reviewed the verses he would preach on the following morning. Sofia usually sat up with him as he prepared his sermons, but tonight she looked particularly tired.

"Why don't you go to bed," he offered. "It's been a hard few days and you need the rest."

"The waiting, Pyotr, I . . ." Her voice trailed off as she leaned against the wall on the other side of the kitchen area. "Yes, perhaps I should get to bed now." Crossing to where her husband sat, she took his hands in hers, pressed them against her face, and muttered something–a short prayer Pyotr assumed–then kissed each of his hands before shuffling off to the bedroom.

Turning back to his work, he read out loud softly to himself:

And these words, which I command thee this day, shall be in thine heart: And thou shalt teach them diligently unto thy children, and shalt talk of them when thou sittest in thine house, and when thou walkest by the way, and when thou liest down, and when thou risest up.

That was all that they wanted to do: teach their children and include them in the worship services that the Soviet Constitution gave them the supposed right to hold. But Yuri and his colleagues at the CRA had very different ideas.

Pyotr thumbed the pages of the Bible gently to turn to another passage but was interrupted by an ear-splitting crash. He looked up just in time to see splinters from the now-shattered apartment door fly past his face.

A startled scream came from the bedroom, followed by the unmistakable cry of terror and anguish from his children who were now awake and aware, even at their young age, of what was happening.

"Papa!"

"Stay where you-" Pyotr tried to yell, but was cut off by a sharp, blinding blow to his cheek. Even before a groan of agonizing pain reached his throat, he felt rough fabric cover his head and large, gloved hands drag him out of his house.

As he regained consciousness, it took Pyotr a moment to realize that the screams coming from somewhere down the hall were not, in fact, those of his wife and children. He felt a pang of shame at the relief he felt knowing that the cries of pain came from an adult he would never know. He whispered a quick prayer for the stranger down the hall and wondered how long it would be until his own ordeal began.

He did not have to wait long to find out. Before he had time to fully grasp the pulsing pain on the side of his head, he heard the door unbolt and open slowly. In stepped Yuri and another man that Pyotr did not recognize. The stranger sat down at the table across from him while Yuri hid himself in the shadows on the far wall.

"Hello, Pyotr," the stranger said, in a voice that seemed altogether too calm. "Yuri tells me that you've been up to . . . interesting things lately."

Pyotr remained silent. He knew, of course, that torture was the threat that lurked beneath the surface of many such interrogations, but he resolved not to speak unless compelled to do so.

"You needn't be worried about me, *Pastor* Pyotr." When he said it, the title dripped with contempt. "Do I look like the sort who would risk bloodying his own fists just to get information?"

The interrogator opened the file and shuffled a few pages. "I don't expect you to tell us the names of those in your church. As you can see, we already know who they are."

Pyotr sighed. Theirs had never been an underground church. He was saddened not so much that his flock was known to the CRA, but that they were now being threatened because of him.

"What we want to know," the interrogator continued, twirling his pencil between his fingers, "is who got to you? Who could so poison the mind of an otherwise obedient pastor such as yourself that you would go along with it? Such information is very useful to the state and the Party, as I'm sure you can understand."

Pyotr knew what all the words meant, but the order in which

they came out of the strange interrogator's mouth seemed to make no sense. He realized quickly that his confusion must have shown on his face.

"Oh, Pyotr," the interrogator shook his head gently, in a perverse imitation of fatherly disapproval. "Now is not the time to play innocent. We know it can only have been outside agitators. It is no more than your patriotic duty to tell us who they are."

Lately, that tactic had been a favorite of the CRA: to position the tender consciences of church members like his in between conflicting duties to state and faith. At this moment, however, he truly had no idea what the man was talking about. He started to turn his palms upward in a visual display of his ignorance and winced as the handcuffs cut into the chafing that had developed on his wrists.

"I teach God's Word with help only from above."

The interrogator scoffed gently underneath his breath and set the pencil down on the table. Closing the folder, he said, "I'm sorry to hear you say that, Pyotr."

Then the interrogator slid his chair back from the table slightly, leaned back, and laced his fingers behind his head. Somehow, that more relaxed posture made him seem more menacing to Pyotr.

"Tell me something else, then. Why would you do it? You know the CRA has banned you from bringing children to your church services. You've done everything we've asked until this."

Pyotr's mind raced. He had had endless debates with himself on this very question before ending up where he was now. To try to distill all of that internal dialogue into something he could spit out in the tense moments of an interrogation seemed impossible.

"Speak, Pyotr," the interrogator said, some of his collected manner seeming to wane. "There's *always* a reason."

"We must obey God rather than men," Pyotr whispered, recalling the words of the Apostle Peter.

"What? Speak up!"

"We must obey God rather than men," he said again, this time with more force and conviction. He looked the interrogator directly in the eyes, just the same way he'd taught Josef to do.

The interrogator sat forward in his seat again.

"We *will* make sure that there are no more men who think such things. Doesn't that frighten you, knowing that no one can rescue you? Not even your precious *Jesus*?"

"Sir, I see no need to answer any more of your questions. My God can rescue me, even from all the powers of the CRA, and the Party, and the state. But even if he does not, I want you to know for certain, that we will not serve your gods or worship the golden statue you set up."

The interrogator screwed up his face in a look that was equal parts confusion and indignation.

"Gods? Golden statue? What in the world are you *talking* about? Have you spent so much time with this Jesus nonsense that it's warped your mind?"

Turning back to look at Yuri for the first time the interrogator indignantly said, "You didn't tell me he was mentally deranged, Yuri! This is no use."

With that, the interrogator snatched his folder from the table and swept out of the room, pausing long enough only to say, "He's yours now."

Yuri remained in the shadows for a long moment, before stepping into the light. Pyotr noticed that his face was red and wondered whether it was embarrassment.

"I told you not to make trouble, Pyotr," he said, leaning on the table with both hands. "Why would you say something so ridiculous!?" slapping the table with his hand.

Pyotr's memory flashed with an image of a Yuri as a schoolboy, berating his classmates for besting him in some playground game. A wave of pity and compassion washed over him. He realized that nothing had really changed for Yuri: he was a Party member now and could back up his threats with overwhelming force; he was still that same angry boy, whose only happiness seemed to sprout from inflicting unhappiness on others. And yet, Yuri here seemed distraught that his old classmate was forcing his hand.

Pyotr pondered telling Yuri the story of the three Jewish boys who stood up to a king—how obedience to their God outweighed all the pain that earthly government powers could threaten them with. But before the words could form on Pyotr's lips, Yuri's heavy fist fell there instead. After the second blow, he felt nothing.

The train was drafty and crowded, but Sofia knew she had no choice. Escape—no, merely the *chance* to escape—was a blessing from God. She had hesitated at first, but her friends prevailed upon her to leave Ulyanovka for the sake of her children, if for no other reason.

Elena amused herself with a doll given to her by an adopted grandfather from church. How much Sofia knew the child would miss him.

"Mama," the little girl said, "will you tell me again why Papa had to go to Jesus?"

"Don't ask stupid questions," interjected Josef, who so far had been the most bitter. "We're not alone on this train-"

"Be quiet, Josef," Sofia scolded mildly. The boy, just turned fifteen, had lost his father at a crucial age and it would do no good to sanction his anger. He sulked, but he obeyed.

"Dear one, as I told you before," she began, smoothing the child's wild, flaxen hair as she talked, "Papa loved Jesus more than anyone or anything."

"More than you, Mama?!"

"Yes, even more than me. But in our country, there are people who cannot accept men like that. That kind of love, they say, belongs to the Party, to the government. I know it's hard to understand at your age."

The girl stroked her doll's hair and tipped up onto her toes to look out the compartment's one, small window. Josef shifted in his seat and crossed his arms. Sofia ignored his thinly-veiled petulance; he needed time. Elena too would be fine eventually, so innocent was her devotion to her father and so full her trust.

Yevgeny, however, worried her. He had always been the brightest of her three children, and yet he had now remained silent for days. Elena's childish inquiries were to be expected; even Josef's stormy sullenness was understandable. But this untouchable distance was almost too much for a mother to bear.

As a bump in the tracks unexpectedly shook them, Sofia noticed a small object fall out of Yevgeny's satchel onto the floor. It bounced across the car to her feet and she picked it up.

"What's this, Zhenya? One of your chess pieces?"

The boy barely nodded as she handed him the piece.

"This one's the bishop, isn't it?" she asked, trying to draw her son out of himself.

He nodded again and stuffed the piece securely in his pocket.

Yevgeny broke his silence a few minutes later, his eyes never leaving the floor. "Mama, how are we to remember Papa?"

"Well, Zhenya," she began, hoping the family nickname might help keep him out of his introversion. "We have all of our memories. We've brought our small photo album-"

"No, that's not what I mean," he interjected, suddenly, yet not angrily. He looked up into his mother's eyes and continued, quite insistently. "I mean was he a *good* man? Why would they do this if he did nothing wrong?"

"They." Sofia realized that even in a lifetime she had not fully plumbed the depths of that single word. "They" were—or so *"they"* said—her Party, her protectors and providers, her government. There was no explanation she could give her son at this moment that would fully satisfy his precociousness. She promised herself that she would make him understand, no matter how long it took.

For now, she settled for cradling his head in her lap as he traced the contours of his chess piece with a sleepy thumb. How fitting to keep the memory of his father, she thought to herself. The bishop.

She whispered softly to him while stroking his young brow,

"Remember him exactly as 'they' saw him, my son. Exactly how your Papa wanted to be known: a man who walked with Christ."

SOMEDAY EVERYWHERE
BY
BILLIE HOLLADAY SKELLEY

"I won't do it. I tell you—I won't!"

"Princess Teresa, as the eldest daughter of the king, it is your responsibility. You are fifteen now, and you know your duty in the matter."

Clenching her fists, as if preparing for a fight, Princess Teresa circled decisive strides around her bed chamber. A scarlet flush rose in her cheeks, and flashes of anger lit her cornflower-blue eyes. She tried to organize her thoughts, but she was too distressed to think logically. The recent news, conveyed by her old, beloved nurse, Eula, had infuriated and unnerved her.

After several turns around the room, Princess Teresa stopped pacing, sighed heavily, and gave in to her frustration. She sat down next to Eula on the silk sofa near the window. Neither woman spoke, but Princess Teresa pondered a resolve to her predicament. Her gaze fell on the worn, weathered face of her elderly companion. Eula had always been there for her, ever since she was a baby, caring for her, teaching her, and supporting her desires and wishes. Even now, Eula's small, grey eyes, almost hidden beneath drooping, wrinkled lids, were full of love and encouragement.

As Princess Teresa carefully studied Eula's face, she realized her old nurse truly thought this news was a good thing—but how could she possibly think so?

With another sigh, Princess Teresa stood up again, leaving Eula on the sofa. She resumed her long strides about the room. With each step, her agitation grew. So many confusing ideas and troubling images were swirling through her head. She needed to find answers, but her unsettled brain kept returning to one thought: *If Eula doesn't understand, what chance do I have of convincing anyone else?*

"My Lady, you should see the occasion as one of rejoicing," Eula declared from her perch on the sofa. "Your marriage to Prince Bellhaven will cement an alliance between our two countries. It is good news. It is a time for celebration."

"Eula, he is ten years my senior. I know nothing about him."

"In time, you will learn."

"What if he hates me?"

"My Lady," Eula beseeched her with hands held together as if in prayer, "you are intelligent, talented, and so beautiful. He will have no choice but to care for you, just as I do..."

"Eula, he knows nothing about me," the princess quickly interjected. "We don't even speak the same language. He doesn't care at all for me. It is a political marriage ... a means to seal a political agreement. Our two countries have been at odds, and now, somehow, I am to be a peace prize. My father is simply making a strategic military and economic alliance. No actual love or caring is involved."

"Nonsense, my Lady, Prince Bellhaven knows you are a royal princess."

"Eula, you don't understand. Political marriages may unite nations, but they rarely involve genuine respect or actual romance. They also rarely last."

"Oh, my Lady, do not think so. Do not say such things. The terms of the marriage have already been negotiated. If you refuse now, your father will be embarrassed and furious."

"But I had no input in the negotiations. I am no more than a piece of property that is being sold. I am being used as currency.

Prince Bellhaven might as well have bought one of my father's renowned horses."

"Don't be foolish, my Lady. You will be happy."

"No, Eula, I won't be happy unless I can do what I want, and what I want is to choose my own husband!"

Eula shuddered as a small gasp escaped her lips. Her eyebrows drew together in a worried frown, and she blinked as a single tear fell on her leathery cheek.

"Don't cry, Eula. It's just … don't you see? How am I to accept this? How can I adapt when there are so many differences between us? It's not just the language. Prince Bellhaven's upbringing, his culture … even his food is different. I know so little about him. Does he read? Will he enjoy my sonatas on the harpsichord? Does he even like music? What about my appearance? Will he consider me beautiful? I have no idea what he even values as beauty."

Regarding the princess carefully, Eula answered in a soft voice, barely above a whisper.

"Attachments are based on more than appearances, my Lady."

"I know, Eula, but we have little upon which to form an attachment. We do not even share the same religious beliefs. I have been raised in the Protestant faith. My obedience is to God. He is a Catholic. The doctrines and practices of his church are so strange and foreign to me."

"He is still a Christian, my Lady."

"Yes, but for me, his church offers no religious appeal and little spiritual comfort. How can my father ask this of me? I have heard him say a hundred times that the Catholic church is corrupt. Yet, he orders me to be married in this church. He demands that I embrace the Catholic doctrines and adhere to the church's teachings. What about my religious liberty?"

"Has it not been said, my Lady, that we should learn about other religions and respect their practices?"

"Learning and respecting are one thing, Eula. Adopting, believing, and following are another. I have no choice in this. I am being forced."

"But, my Lady, I believe you can carry the spirit of your faith with you wherever you go. For the sake of appearances, you may have to worship in his church and practice his religious rituals, but in your heart, you can believe as you wish. There is a certain freedom of thought within one's being. I mean your personal relationship with God need not change."

"I see, Eula. I just have to pretend. I must live a lie."

"No, my Lady, I did not mean that."

Princess Teresa continued pacing around the room. The color in her cheeks had deepened.

"Eula, I want to marry someone who shares my values, my beliefs, and my religion. I want to marry someone I care about and love. I also want him to care about me and love me."

Eula winced and shook her head in exasperation.

"My Lady ... my Lady, you must not say such things. It will only lead to trouble."

"What I want does not matter," continued Princess Teresa. "It is no use. I am trapped. I see now, Eula, that from the day I was born, my life has been a continuum of coercion ... from everyone ... even you."

Eula gasped. "No, my Lady, no!" she beseeched her charge plaintively.

"Yes, Eula, and if you thought about it, you'd admit it," the princess said as she paused in thought. "Since I was a child, there have been forces propelling me down this path. The stories told to me as a child ... my schooling ... a word here or there from family members ... all efforts to guide my thoughts and affect my position. It has all been part of a prearranged plan to compel me to comply in marriage, hasn't it?!" Princess Theresa demanded as she resumed her pacing.

Eula lowered her head and nervously began wringing her hands.

"It is true, Eula. All my life, there have been subtle influences ... familial, social, cultural, civic ... even religious ... pressuring me to do what is best for the court and the country. All these efforts have been directed at instilling concepts of self-denial, obedience to my parents, the greater good, and my duty. Always ... always, there is my duty. Say it is not so, Eula!"

Eula straightened and raised her tone. "Do not say such things, my Lady. They will say you are spoiled and self-centered to put your own ideas and desires above your family's position and your country's welfare."

"Eula, it is more than that ... don't you see? For the first time, I realize I have no autonomy. I have no freedom. I'm not sure I've ever had any. I ... I should like to argue my position, to protest this coercion, but it would be no use .... I have no standing to voice anything. Equality is a word that doesn't apply to me. I am the daughter of a king, but as a woman, I have no rights."

Eula pointed a knotted finger at the young princess whom she had raised since birth. "You are obligated, my Lady, to respect your father's wishes," she scolded. "If you break the marriage contract, it will bring shame to your father, your family, and your country. It could even lead to war. Your father will be angry and disappointed, and he will take his displeasure out on you. He will send you away. You will have to stay hidden from the world. I shall never see you again."

Princess Teresa paused abruptly in her pacing to consider Eula's words. As she stood motionless, weighing her options, the light dimmed in her eyes and the color in her face paled. After several minutes, she spoke again.

"Yes, Eula, I see my choices are limited ... but I have one other option. I could end it myself. I could ... I mean ... I might be better off dead."

"Oh, Princess Teresa, not suicide! No, a thousand times no. It accomplishes nothing. You must think clearly. Your death would solve nothing. Your father would still be aggrieved. He would still be indebted to Prince Bellhaven and his country, and there still could be war."

"Yes, I know ... but at least I'd be free."

"No, my Lady, I won't hear you speak so."

Covering her eyes with her wrinkled hands, Eula crumbled and began to cry again.

Princess Teresa sat down once more on the sofa beside Eula. She gathered the old woman's wrinkled hands in her smooth, young ones, and they sat in silence for several minutes.

Suddenly, Princess Teresa rose from the sofa and walked quickly toward her bed on the other side of the chamber. The safety of the richly-embroidered curtain panels hanging from the ornamental canopy seem to beckon to her. She ran her fingers along the soft fabric of these panels, taking comfort in their familiarity. Changing her focus from the fabric to the bed itself, she shook her head and sighed deeply at something unseen in the bed. Her countenance suddenly shifted from defiant warrior to defeated captive.

Mentally exasperated and physically exhausted, Princess Teresa lay down upon the bed's silk coverlet.

Eula slowly rose from the sofa and followed the path of Princess Teresa's footsteps to the bed. Gently, she sat down on the side of the bed, next to the princess.

Once again, silence reigned. For several minutes, neither woman seemed certain of what to say. Finally, in a voice Eula thought unnatural and distant, Princess Teresa spoke.

"Religions give people a purpose and a framework for their lives. They provide a sense of belonging. I understand this, Eula, and I accept that no one religion holds all the answers. I can adapt, as you indicated, and still keep my personal relationship with God."

Eula's face darkened in concern at the sound of this strange, steely voice.

"I am confident," the princess continued, "the basic doctrines of my faith, taught to me as a child, will remain with me wherever I go. My religion is important to me, but, as you indicated, Eula, I can learn to worship publicly one way and privately still maintain my own beliefs. Perhaps, I am more of a spiritual person, than a truly religious one."

"I think, my Lady, you are both religious and spiritual," Eula offered.

"One of my teachers," continued Princess Teresa, "told me a long time ago that devoutly religious people follow the doctrines and tenets of their particular religion. They do what their religion says, no matter what is right. Spiritual people, on the other hand, do what is right–no matter what their religion dictates."

Confused, Eula did not respond. Nervously, she began stroking the soft edge of the bed's coverlet.

"I think, Eula, that may be my problem. I like to think for myself. I want to do what I believe is fair and just ... and a big part of me wants terribly to fight the injustice of this forced marriage."

"But, my Lady," said Eula, looking up to meet Princess Teresa's eyes, "you don't have to brandish a sword to fight injustice. Many people have engaged in nonviolent struggles against all kinds of tyranny."

"Ah, Eula, we're back to pretending and quietly living that lie."

Eula blushed and lowered her eyes back to the coverlet.

"I think," Princess Teresa continued, "individuals should have the right to make their own choice in a companion ... and romantic attraction and religious beliefs should be part of that consideration. I understand, however, my father's wishes and the law of the land ... but I tell you, Eula ... on this day, I also will make a law unto myself. Outwardly, I will do what is demanded of me. I will act as expected. Inwardly, however, I will think and believe as I wish."

"But, my Lady," Eula stopped short as her gaze fell on the face of Princess Teresa.

The young princess' lively countenance had vanished. Her face, white as death, now seemed carved from wood. An emptiness had settled in her eyes.

Eula gave a little gasp at the sight. Her eyes widened in concern.

"Do not worry, Eula. As the king's daughter, I know my responsibility in the matter. I will do my duty and marry Prince Bellhaven. I will live the lie. They may make the rules and demand my compliance to them, but they cannot rule my spirit. I will think what I wish and believe what I want ... and I believe, Eula, that one day ... all women ... everywhere ... will be able to govern their own fate. They will be free to choose their own husbands and free to worship as they wish. One day, women will be able to make their own decisions. Someday ... someday, the world will be different ... women will have rights. They will be able to make their own choices and control their own lives. Someday, Eula, someday."

2019: THE AFRICAN CONTINENT
(Three Hundred Years Later)

"I won't do it. I tell you I won't."

"Adaeze, you are fifteen years old and your father's eldest daughter. You must do what he says. As the chief of our people, he knows what is best."

Standing beneath a marula tree, not far from their village, Adaeze and her grandmother, Mariama, faced each other as if ready for combat. Words seemed to have temporarily failed them, and they faced-off in stony silence.

Frustrated and angry, Adaeze stared defiantly at the coppery, wrinkled face of her grandmother. In the shade of the tree, Mariama's weathered brow and ebony eyes appeared particularly dark and hostile.

Mariama, in turn, glared at the youthful face of her granddaughter. A bronze glow, radiating from Adaeze's cheeks, seemed to highlight her wild and untamed spirit. The light flashing in Adaeze's dark eyes appeared to Mariama to reflect her granddaughter's stubborn determination. Adaeze had always exhibited strength of character, but today her courage and fortitude were clearly on display.

Mariama elected to end the silent standoff.

"We should be celebrating, not fighting, Adaeze. Your marriage to your cousin, Shehu, will strengthen our family ties and combine the prosperity of both our families."

"You mean by marrying him," retorted Adaeze, "that I will be unable to enter an unsuitable relationship or get pregnant out of wedlock and bring shame on the family."

"Be careful what you say, Granddaughter. You must think. It is your father's duty to select your husband, and he has selected a good man."

"Shehu is ten years older than me, Mariama. We are not alike at all. Our customs are not the same. I love school. Shehu doesn't attend school. I have spent my entire life in the Apostolic church. I believe in prayer and the teachings of the apostles. You know I am a Christian. Shehu ... Shehu practices the Animist religion. He follows traditional practices ... the old indigenous faith. He believes, Mariama, if he breaks a taboo or violates a rule of his people, it will cause him hardship and illness. He thinks he will be cursed! To atone for such violations, he makes blood sacrifices ... sacrifices to restore the harmony in his life!"

"This matters not, as you know. Your husband may do as he likes."

Adaeze flashed a look of disgust in her grandmother's direction, but if Mariama saw this look, she did not acknowledge it. Instead, the old woman stared off at the blue haze circling the distant hills.

Adaeze turned away. She looked longingly the other direction toward her village, the only home she had ever known. *How can it be*, she thought, *that Mariama does not understand? This is the woman who has cared for me since I was a baby. She has fed me, watched over me, and taught me about life. She knows me better than any living being. How is it possible she does not understand my position now?*

Turning back, Adaeze faced her grandmother. She had to try again to explain.

"Mariama, Shehu and I have nothing in common. He follows the old ways ... performing ritualistic trances, ceremonies, and sacrifices. His ways are not wrong, for him ... but I cannot worship inanimate objects, like trees and stones. Do you honestly think I should join him in seeking spiritual guidance from a lion or a water-spirit? Shehu believes he must regularly honor his ancestors with rituals and gifts. He looks to them for guidance."

"It would do you no harm, Adaeze, to learn to honor your relatives."

"I do honor my relatives, but that does not mean I have to pray to them. It does not mean I have to worship my ancestors and build shrines to them!"

"As I have said and as you know, your husband may do as he wishes."

"Yes, Grandmother, I know. Shehu may choose his religion. It is his choice, and as you say, he may do as he wishes ... but why do I have to embrace and follow his beliefs?"

"How many times has my father said we should give up the old ways and live in the new world? He teaches me one thing and tells me to practice another. How can he ask this of me?"

Again, Adaeze turned away from her grandmother's piercing stare. She had to figure out her confusing dilemma.

Think, she told herself. *What choices do I have? What can I do? I might try to protest the situation ... in front of the whole village. I could ask other girls to join my protest ... but ... but the chances of attracting anyone to my cause are small. Assembling resistance of any kind would be difficult. There are girls who might want to join me, but they would be forbidden by their families ... forcibly if necessary. No, that would only lead to them being harmed or confined. My protest would bring dishonor to my family. I ... I could run away and try to hide in a women's shelter in the city ... but then what? If anyone from my family or Shehu's family found me in such a place, it would be bad. Yes, if they caught me, it would be very bad.*

Adaeze made a furtive glance at her grandmother's face. *Did Mariama know what she was thinking?*

Before Adaeze could decide regarding her grandmother's thoughts, the old woman spoke again.

"You think and speak nonsense, Adaeze. You are a smart girl and a good daughter. You know it is your duty to obey your father."

"Can't you see, Mariama? Being smart or good doesn't matter. Nothing that I do or think matters. I don't matter. I am powerless. What choice do I have?"

Mariama did not answer, but her face darkened with anger.

Mariama will be of no help, Adaeze thought. *There is no one to help me. I am trapped. There is nothing I can do.*

Looking into Mariama's eyes, Adaeze spoke softly and carefully.

"Grandmother, I understand. I know if I don't marry Shehu, you and father will be shamed, and Shehu's family will be insulted."

As soon as the words passed her lips, the light went out in Adaeze's eyes. She suddenly recalled hearing about another girl, from a neighboring village, who had refused an arranged marriage. The groom's family had felt insulted. They had killed the girl to erase the affront to their dignity.

Would Shehu's family murder me? Yes, it is a definite possibility, Adaeze realized.

As she weighed her options again, Adaeze felt more and more that the situation was hopeless. Confused and frustrated, she felt compelled to try once more to make her grandmother understand.

"Mariama … please … don't you see what it means? If I marry Shehu, I will have few rights and little freedom. He may not even let me finish school. In all things, I will be subordinate to him. I am being forced into a form of slavery … marital slavery."

"You show your youth and your foolishness, Adaeze. You have a duty and you must do your duty." Softening a little at her granddaughter's obvious distress, Mariama added, "But remember, you can always keep your own feelings and beliefs hidden in your heart. In your own mind, you can still think and believe as you wish."

"You want me to live a lie. To believe one thing and do another. Yes, I can keep my thoughts hidden … and live like I'm not alive … just shifting in the shadows day after day."

Feeling disrespected, Mariama returned to the offensive.

"You must do what your father says. I know you do not believe it, but if you refuse your father's wishes, you will be cursed."

"I am cursed already, Mariama," Adaeze proclaimed in disgust. She left the shade of the marula tree and walked into sunlight. Normally she drew strength from the sun's strong rays, but today she felt its heat was wilting her mind and body.

Think, she told herself again. *There must be other options.*

Slowly an idea took root in her brain.

I could … I could kill myself. I know I could do it … I could … but to what end? Death would provide my personal escape, but I still would be disgracing my family. Even death is not an answer. I am powerless. There is nothing I can do. I have no choice. I have no autonomy. I have no freedom to conduct myself as I wish. I am lost.

Slowly, Adaeze returned to the shade of the marula tree. A steely resolve now filled her dark eyes, and the features of her face were set, as if carved from stone. Her voice was clear and strong, but it seemed to arise from far-away in the distant hills.

"I see now, Mariama, that I was born into a trap from which there is no escape. There is no freedom for me. I was raised to be a slave to my husband. I have no rights, no autonomy, and no liberty. I know my duty, and I will do my duty. I will marry Shehu, as you and father wish. I will live the lie. You and Father may force me to comply, but I think, someday, the world will be different. Someday all women everywhere will have rights. They will be able to make their own decisions regarding their husband, their religion, and their life. They will be able to choose their own destiny. Someday, Mariama, someday."

Adaeze spoke in earnest to appease Mariama, but she knew in her heart she could not comply. That evening, when night fell on the village, she ran–intent on escaping the forced marriage to Shehu whatever the cost.

For days she kept moving farther and farther away from her village. With each step, she vowed to be an instrument of change.

"The only way to change something is to act," she told herself. "Words alone are not enough. I will act, and I'll work to reverse this trend of young girls being forced into early marriages. Someday has to be today."

PROMISES KEPT
BY
N.B. WILLIAMS

Vercingetorix looked at the tattered cloth in his hands and felt his elation build. The weave was tight and the color was the vaunted Tyrian purple the Romans loved so well. Connected as he was to the earth through the battle-spell cast by the Morrigan, he could feel the pain of the thousand snails that died to color that scrap of cloth. His broad fingers closed upon it, crushing it as the Roman craftsmen crushed the shells of the mollusks they sacrificed for their rare coloration. This cloth belonged to a noble, one he would delight in grinding beneath his heel until his blood dyed the earth. He grinned at the irony.

He'd been chasing Iulius Caesar for years, beating back his legions again and again as they strove to subdue the wild Kells that populated the dark forests of Gaul. Every time he managed to decimate them and force a retreat, the Romans simply sent more troops from their home city, making it just a matter of time before they prodded their swords into Kellic territories again.

Vercingetorix dropped the cloth into a wooden bowl near the hearth. The Morrigan could use it to help locate the commander, after which he would formulate a plan to slip inside the Roman encampment and put an end to his sworn enemy. *Cut off the head of the snake*, he thought, *and the body dies.*

"Or three heads grow in its place."

Vercingetorix whirled, his dagger drawn. In the doorway stood a woman, jet black hair curling from under a helmet crested with stiffened horsehair. On her shoulder, a heart-faced owl regarded him with solemn eyes.

"Who dares cross my threshold without permission?" His voice shook with anger, but the woman appeared nonplussed by his surfeit of emotion, her gray eyes watching him with mild amusement.

"I think, Son of Kells, that you'd best ask your Morrigan for guidance before insulting goddesses who come to offer aid." The tall woman stepped aside, and Vercingetorix saw the lithe figure of the Morrigan standing in the mists beyond the door. His eyes shifted from woman to woman, but he remained motionless, crouched in a fighting stance.

The Morrigan moved forward, head bent in deference to the warrior-goddess. "You must apologize and make amends to Minerva, for she has come to offer her help."

Vercingetorix' face showed no emotion, but he sheathed his dagger.

"Minerva? She's a Roman deity—why would she deign help our cause?" He kept his dark eyes on the bright figure of the goddess and on her owl as it clacked its beak at him and hissed.

Minerva put a hand on the Morrigan's shoulder. "Be at ease, sister. I don't blame your warrior for being skeptical. After all, with my help the Romans have managed to keep him and his unwashed tribes at bay for many years, outsmarting and outwitting them at every turn."

Vecingetorix's face flushed red and he ground his square teeth together. "Why, you–," The Morrigan shot him a black look and shook her head in warning. With great effort he swallowed his anger and pride and simply glared, waiting for one of the women to make the next move.

Minerva smiled, her thin lips forming the perfect shape of a hunter's bow. "I will excuse your rudeness for I can see your warrior's heart cannot help but leap at the chance to fight, an attribute I highly esteem." Here she paused, giving her owl's head a scratch while she let her words sink in. "But you would be wise to hold your tongue."

Vercingetorix could see the Morrigan staring, eyes gleaming through their kohl-rimmed lids. He could feel the push of her magick, the tendrils of her will twining their way through the folds of his mind, seeking to control his emotions. He swatted at his head, shaking it like a horse when its nose has been stung by a fly.

"Stop!" he said to no one in particular. The goddesses exchanged knowing glances, Minerva's enigmatic smile still hovering on her lips.

"Be at ease, warrior," she said, striding into the room to take a seat on the one chair available. "I'm here to offer you my help against Caesar's legions. I love strategy, and for this reason the Romans have had my assistance against you Kells, who fight with the wildness of beasts, all rage and no reason." She noted the tell-tale signs of irritation, the stiffening of his shoulders and the clenching of his jaw, but it was promising that he made no effort to defend himself. "What I do *not* love is my brother Mars' keen appreciation for bloodshed and murder. It's one thing to conquer a people through superior maneuvering and tactics. It's another to slaughter them for the sheer joy of it." She eyed him as he continued to stand in silence.

"What is your wish, goddess?" he said, with as much humility as he could muster.

Her lips quirked at his discomfiture. Obviously, civility was not his usual means of expression.

"I am going to end these Kellic wars once and for all and I'm going to help you to victory to do it. Iulius Caesar is on the move to a town called Gergovia. I want you to gather up your tribesmen and encamp on the high ground. Caesar will try to surround you and force you into open battle, but in doing so, he'll run out of supplies. When he does, you'll strike–and be victorious." She sat back in the chair, forcing the owl to step forward to avoid catching his talons between her shoulder and the chair back.

"And then?" Vercingetorix hadn't remained alive in this brutal land by simply accepting what he was told.

Minerva tilted her head. "Then you live to fight again, King of Kells. You'll have one more battle to command against this Iulius, and to do it you'll unite the whole of Kellic society under one mantle–yours."

King of Kells. Vercingetorix let his mind wander over the possibilities. A stable society could begin to produce material goods for trade. Trade would mean wealth. Wealth would be shared among the community and, of course, their king. He saw himself upon a carved throne, a beautiful queen by his side, a feast-table laden with delicacies from the four corners of his vast kingdom. His mouth watered.

Finally feeling full enough of his own destiny to be able to show appropriate homage to the goddess, he bowed. "Thank you, Minerva, for your confidence and your help. I'll not disappoint you."

Minerva stood and inclined her head to him, the red horsehair of her helmet trembling with the movement. "Take care, warrior. The Romans are still a formidable enemy for you –even with the help of an immortal." She trailed a finger across his cheek as she swept out the door, leaving him feeling weak as he watched her form fade into the mists of the forests like a breath dissolves in the cold air of winter.

The Morrigan stood in the doorway, her sullen expression leaving no wonder as to her feelings.

"You are an impudent fool," she said bluntly. "Their goddess of tact and strategy wants to assist you and you act like a boorish, egotistical swine? What were you thinking?" Her eyes blazed and her dark hair writhed around her head, a dark halo in the mist.

"I have *you*, Morrigan. You're also a deity of battle: wilder, rampant, and more savage than the Roman gods. We've held our own so far; there's no reason to think we wouldn't keep on holding it, even without Minerva's help. And, my people are consecrated to you and all that you represent. When I agreed to lead them, I called for an accord that any Kell in my service would dedicate his–and his family's–life to your worship.

"Fool!" she spat. "Are you content with just 'holding on'? Is that all you aspire to? Minerva is offering you victory. Absolute victory," she cocked her head to the side in that birdlike way of hers and added, "And a throne."

He waved a hand in her face. "Of course I see the benefit of her alliance. Don't be stupid. But we don't *need* it. We *want* it."

"Don't speak like that!" The Morrigan spit on the earth and rubbed her saliva into the dirt with her toe, as if erasing something. "This is a *goddess* you treat with, one older and more powerful than I. You don't bargain with a goddess, human fool. And," she whispered, "if any of your Kells should choose to follow her, you should allow it."

Vercingetorix laughed softly, shaking his head in the negative, and sitting in his chair which still held the warmth from Minerva's body. The heat made him oddly uncomfortable and in a moment he was up, ushering the Morrigan out into the forest and rousing his tribesmen from their mud and wattle homes to prepare their battle plan.

They won Gergovia as Minerva had promised and the Kellic army marched on to the hilltop town of Alesia, a high ground that was easily defended. Along the way, a small contingent of his troops–troops who should be honoring the Morrigan–begged Vercingetorix to perform sacrifices to Minerva out of respect for her, and to ensure her goodwill in the future. After placing more than one stripe on the backs of men who refused to honor the Morrigan, he set about grumbling that Minerva had not yet fulfilled her promise to make him king.

The Morrigan cringed at his words and warned him to keep the faith with the goddess–and to allow his men to worship where they would.

"She is a goddess, Lord. She's not to be played with and discarded as if you were playing a game of *latrone*." The tendrils of her hair rose up and surrounded her face, writhing in concert with her irritation like shiny black snakes. "You need to show respect. And, if she holds the hearts of some of your men, so be it. I am not a jealous deity."

Vercingetorix sneered. "The worship of those men is worthless, as they so easily change their allegiance from you to her. And remember, Morrigan. Minerva came to *me*. I did not invoke her name or ask for her help."

"No, but you accepted it. You are bound. She will require you to hand over that which belongs to her –the hearts of her faithful." She paused, adding, "And men's hearts should be free to worship the deity that matters to them. The one that sets their hearts on fire. The one that causes them to be their best self. It matters not whether it is me, Minerva, or some other god or goddess."

He smiled, a thin stretch of his lips that contained little humor. "She is also bound. An immortal may not take back her word. And, as for her faithful –they are human men and women and, as such, they are pledged to me. I command their worship, and right now I insist that they worship *you*. Why would you have a problem with that?"

The Morrigan shuddered. This man would taunt a *goddess*? Then there was nothing she could do but let destiny overtake him. With a shake of her snaky locks she left him to make what plans he could for his defense.

With the Kells inside, Caesar ordered his troops to construct a wall of timber and earth around the city that completely enclosed it, hoping to starve them out. During construction, Vercingetorix sent constant raids of warriors that attempted to break through to fetch reinforcements, but he was unsuccessful until the wall was nearly complete.

The day the Roman contingent were finishing the final earthen panel, a group of Kells on horseback came screaming through the men, some slashing with short swords, others firing arrows. With a combination of shock and awe, they managed to break free of the encircling wall and gallop off into the distance.

Caesar was no fool. He knew the escaped Kells were capable of mustering thousands more wild warriors to their cause. Vercingetorix was related to most of the Kellic chieftains–if anyone could unite them, he could. Caesar was tired and his men demoralized. He wished to conquer these feral people and return to Rome and his family, tired of this senseless bloodshed that moved neither army closer to victory.

One evening after he'd instructed his generals on the morrow's maneuvers, he retreated to his private sanctuary, a tent replete with all the luxuries that could be afforded on campaign –carpets, a sturdy oak bed with feathered mattress and fine woolen blankets, a hearth bowl with a cheery fire and an altar table for worship.

Caesar fell to his knees at the altar table, knocking his forehead thrice against the edge in frustration. Then from his pocket he drew an owl feather and placed it with care in the table's center. Next, he drew his *pugio* and, with no hesitation, used it to slash his hand across the meaty part of the palm, letting the blood drip in scarlet dribbles onto the feather where it pooled.

"Oh Minerva, Goddess of Wisdom! Hear your supplicant, who has always been true. I seek to win, but I would do it with wisdom, with tactics, and not with bloodshed. I call upon you, Minerva, to bestow your wisdom upon me that I may prevail!"

He lowered himself to the floor, lying prostrate at the foot of the table, his hand throbbing where he'd cut it. After a moment, he heard the flapping of wings and a sandaled foot appeared at his head.

"Get up, Iulius, and look upon me." Minerva touched her foot to his hand and immediately the blood ceased to flow and the edges of wounded skin knit together. He got to his feet, keeping eyes averted.

"Minerva." It was all he could manage. He'd never imagined the goddess herself would pay him a visit. His heart, so valiant in battle, beat like a *tympanum* in his chest as he struggled with what to say. How exactly did one address a goddess?

Minerva smiled at his agitation. "You may look upon me, Iulius, as I have a gift to bestow upon you for your–," she cast her hand at the altar where the feather, white as bone, floated upon its bloody sea, "–loyalty and sacrifice."

He raised his dark eyes to her face, fearful that the radiance of a goddess would blind him. Instead, he saw a handsome woman with clear gray eyes studying him with no small amusement. She was tall, yes, and muscled. But other than the owl that sat astride her shoulder, she looked no different from any other woman. He let himself relax.

The goddess smiled. "See? I am here to help you, Consul. I wish you to be victorious in this battle, so I will give you the strategy you need to win."

He nodded, eagerness shining in his eyes.

"You must build a second wall, outside of the first. A contravallation, I believe it's called. Place your entire encampment between the walls. When the Kells' reinforcements come, leave your infantry to defend the outer wall and lead the cavalry through a break in it to surround the Kells from the outside."

Caesar frowned. "But they can attack us from both sides, then. From the city to the inner wall *and* from the outer wall."

Minerva nodded. "This is so. But Vercingetorix and his men are weakened by starvation. It has been months since the troops have gotten food past the wall. Their resistance will be puny. As for the others, you will surprise them with the attack from behind and there are no more reinforcements to be had. This is the sum total of their resistance."

Caesar considered her plan from all angles and found it perfect. He was a brilliant general and with no small expertise at tactics, but her strategy was unassailable. He fell to his knees.

"Oh, Goddess! Thank you for sharing your Wisdom with me. I will follow your instruction to the letter and pray to see you again on the day of victory."

Minerva ruffled the feathers on her owl's head. "My dear Consul, I shall look forward to it."

When he looked up again, she had gone. A bright object gleaming on the carpet caught his eye. Another owl feather, pristine white with a silver vein down the center, lay where she had been standing. He picked it up, tucking it in his pocket for luck.

In a month, the relief army commanded by Vercassivellaunos, Vercingetorix' cousin, arrived at Alesia. The wild band of warriors stormed the Roman wall, setting fire to the timbers and trying to climb the earthen sides. Vercingetorix, seeing his cousin's army hammering away at Caesar's defenses, called his troops to rain arrows on the Roman infantry to distract them from the outside attackers. Quickly, the Romans erected an awning made of tent material that protected them from the arrows while they beat back the attackers from beyond.

Meanwhile, Caesar gathered his cavalry and led them quietly to a small gap in the wall that had been hidden behind some stationary timbers. Unknowingly, Vercingetorix had offered them the perfect subterfuge. The tents erected to stop the arrows also hid the horsemen from view of the city's defenders.

Caesar lined up the men in a column so that once the timbers were removed, the troops could burst through the wall and make their way to the back of the Kellic infantry, with no time for Vercingetorix to alert his cousin of their move.

At his signal, Caesar's horseman flew through the opening, a stream of armed men on horseback plunging wildly toward their enemy. When Vercassivellaunos caught sight of the six thousand horsemen, he sounded the battle horn and rallied his troops. They ceased the siege on the wall and turned to face the Roman cavalry.

Line after line of Kells fell to the swords of the Romans, whose mounted positions lent them the upper hand in the skirmish. Finally, the Kells could hold their position no more.

"Retreat!" screamed Vercassivellaunos as the rest of the men in his army broke and ran for the distant woods and safety.

Vercingetorix watched in disbelief from the ramparts of Alesia, his men panicking as they saw their hope fleeing from battle.

"Morrigan!" he screamed, looking for her flowing capes. "*Morrigan!*"

"Do not scream at me, Lord," she said mildly, appearing like a shadow at his side.

He grabbed her arm and squeezed. "Do something! You're the goddess of battle! Ride among them, bolster their courage, put the berserk upon them!"

She pulled her arm from his grasp "You do not command me. The spirit of the Kellic people commands me, and, regardless of your rules and your regulations, many of their hearts are with Minerva, not with me," she said, narrowing her dark eyes. "Even if I wished to help, I cannot."

He clenched his jaw in anger and his hands fisted at his sides, though he dared not raise them. "*Minerva.* She said I would be victorious. She said I would be king. She *lied!*" He spat those final words out as if ridding his mouth of a bad taste. In a fit of anger, he swept a line of arrows from the parapet and watched them fall, useless, to the tented roofs below. Then he tossed his own shield over the edge, watching as it bounced down the hill and into the Roman encampment.

"I never said you'd be king, though you yet may bear that title." Minerva appeared at his side, her owl poised, wings out, in a menacing stance on her shoulder.

He whirled to face the goddess. "*You*. You promised me victory!"

Minerva's gray eyes clouded. "And victory you had. Did you not win at Gergovia?"

He opened his mouth to reply but she stopped him. "I promised you *a* victory. Not *the* victory. Perhaps, if you'd been more . . . *respectful*, had allowed my fervent followers to worship as they would instead of proscribing their faith–perhaps then that could have been arranged." She gave him a sidelong glance as she preened her owl's feathers. "But it matters not. My goal was simply to stop the Kellic wars, which this battle shall do nicely. And," she said pointedly, "I have not gone back on any of my promises."

Vercingetorix' face was so red it looked like it might burst open like a rotted melon. "How can you say that when all is in ruins at my feet? How–"

A soldier interrupted him. Injured and bleeding, he threw himself on the ground in front of his commander. "Lord," he said, through gasping breaths. "The men wish to surrender. It is our only hope. The Romans have run off our rescuers and we are starving and wounded. They will kill us all if they storm the wall now. We cannot defend it."

Vercingetorix looked at the young man prostrate before him. He probably had a wife and children somewhere in the Kellic woods, burning offerings to Minerva while waiting for him to come home. Or, perhaps he had parents needing their son to come back to the fields in time to help with the harvest. Vercingetorix turned from the wall, finally seeing the pleading hope written large on the faces of his men as they waited for his answer. They were dirty, skinny, and tired. They had fought the good fight and just wanted to go home.

Forgetting his anger, he gave a weary sigh. He had overplayed his hand. If only he hadn't forced the men to sacrifice to the Morrigan when their hearts were not in it. If only he hadn't tried to bend men's free will to his own idea of strength, cunning, and liberty. If only he'd stepped back and looked at the bigger picture, they might have been victorious. Knowing it was his duty to save as many of his men as he could, he made the hard choice. If by his surrender he could preserve their lives, he would.

"Tell the men to send a courier to Caesar. I wish to surrender." The young man nodded and scrambled to his feet without even a word of thanks. Vercingetorix watched him race down the cobbles to the lower city where he could raise a flag of truce to take him through the wall. He saw the white flag unfurl and followed it as it made its way through the mass of Roman soldiers busily dismantling the tenting they no longer needed.

He turned back to Minerva, but she was gone and only the Morrigan, dark and brooding, stood by his side. She touched his arm.

"You do the right thing, Lord. Saving the men." She cocked her head. "Would that you had given them the freedom to choose where to worship and whom to honor from the beginning. If you had, this might not have happened. Nonetheless," she intoned, pointing one long nail at the gray sky. "It is honorable."

He scowled at her and shrugged off her touch. *Honorable, perhaps. But shameful. So shameful.*

Caesar led Vercingetorix to the forum as a prisoner of war as part of his triumphal procession. The vast crowd was animated, and they roared with excitement at each new grandiose display. There was chariot-racing and an elephant fight with twenty beasts per side. Then, a military reenactment with thousands of foot soldiers opposing each other and even a naval battle was performed. This was followed by music and juggling and the distribution of coin to all the soldiers that fought alongside him.

When it came time to display the prisoners, Caesar kept Vercingetorix for last. As the Kellic chieftain mounted the steps he saw on the faces of the crowd not awe, but derision. They hooted at him and threw whatever they could find in his direction until Caesar called for order.

Silence fell as Caesar reached the podium. The crowd held its collective breath, waiting to be addressed by the man who'd conquered not one, but four civilizations during his time as Consul. The air was stifling in the arena and the closeness of thousands of people added to the swelter. Vercingetorix had been cleaned, fed, and given new clothes of Kellic origin to wear. Caesar wanted him to look as exotic as possible to the people of Rome.

He was brought forward, held between two centurion guards, as Caesar spoke. "People of Rome. I give you Vercingetorix, King of Kells!" A swell of applause and the roar of approval from thousands of Roman throats echoed through the arena. The sun was in Vercingetorix' face, so he could see only those closest to the dais. As his eyes roamed over the sunburnt faces raised to him in a mixture of ecstasy and bloodlust, he caught sight of a dark-haired woman in a white chiton standing to the side. She had a silver owl pin on her shoulder and her gray eyes regarded him with sadness.

The noise of the crowd was deafening, but even through it he heard her voice, as if in his head. "You are a King, Vercingetorix. My promises are all kept." Tears welled in his eyes, stinging as he blinked them away. When his vision cleared, the woman was gone and, in her place, stood the Morrigan, a blue hood hiding her snaky hair from the jostling spectators. She, too, looked at him with pity before turning and making her way through the crowd.

Vercingetorix was led away with the other prisoners to await their fate tethered to one another on the dais while Caesar gloried in the adulation of the crowd. Coins and flowers rained down upon the populace and people strained to catch a keepsake from this day of glory. Caesar watched with pride, a father returning home with presents for his children, before silencing them again.

"People of Rome," his strong voice pushed through the warm air, "I will not destroy these captive men, for they have much strength that can be put to use for our fair city." The crowd murmured their dissatisfaction. They had been hoping for bloodsport. Caesar continued, "Our victories were directed by the gods. No matter which gods you worship, by your prayers we were saved. Our Rome, a beacon of freedom and of prosperity, was saved by each and every one of you." He paused as the crowd roared their agreement. As they calmed, he began again, more quietly. "For myself, I have prayed to Minerva for this victory and I would like to honor her for her kindness to us." More murmurs, now interested. "I will build a temple to Minerva in the center of the city. And these men," he swept his arms wide to encompass the prisoners, "shall be the ones to carve and set every stone. Day by day they shall toil in the hot sun and feel the bite of winter until they have raised such a shining monument to Minerva as the world has never known!" The crowd began to cheer, but Caesar put his hand up to stay them. "And afterward, they shall serve as our first sacrifice to her honor!" With that, the crowd went wild, screaming their approval for their new, bold Consul, for their gods, and for the glory and freedom Rome offered her citizens.

Vercingetorix closed his eyes against the irony of his fate as a lone, white feather drifted from the sky to settle gently on the top of his leathern boot, its silver vein shining in the sun.

BINDING CONTRACT
BY
BLAKE JESSOP

CANAAN, 600 B.C.

Abraham and Sarah arrived home early from the dusty fields of Canaan with their son in tow. Isaac was a good boy, a gift from God, and very perceptive.

"We have a visitor," Isaac said. Abraham trusted his son's keen senses.

"Then go to the stores and bring what wine and preserves we have. Sarah, after we greet our guest, whoever he may be, prepare a meal."

Sarah sighed and opened the door to the hut. At their low table sat a striking young Canaanite with short hair, a slim profile and clear blue eyes. None of these features drew so much attention, however, as the pair of tall, neatly folded wings.

"What a beautiful young man," Abraham said, "Surely, you are a messenger from God!"

Sarah sighed again, and said over her shoulder, "we must treat this angel well, husband, I'm sure *she* has flown a long way to find us."

"Indeed," Abraham blinked at the angel. "Have you a message from our Lord?"

"I do," the angel said, giving her hair a self-conscious tug and clearing her throat. "You must listen well and think clearly. God has a request, and I am to set it out before you."

Sarah came and sat, laying out cups and a plate of succulent dates. The angel looked momentarily relieved; it was the first time she had ever delivered such a serious test. She drank a little water to moisten her lips.

"Leave us, wife. This is grave talk," Abraham said. Sarah looked annoyed. The angel shrugged apologetically. It made her wings rustle. When Sarah had grudgingly withdrawn a few steps, the angel spoke.

"Abraham," she recited, "take your son, your only son Isaac, whom you love, and go to the land of Moriah, and offer him there as a burnt offering on one of the mountains that I shall show you. This is the demonstration of faith that your God asks of you. Will you obey him?"

Both Abraham and Sarah gasped. The angel looked concerned and a little nervous.

"If I must," Abraham said, with a heavy heart. "God gave me this son that I did not expect, and it is his right to take him back again. I will begin packing, but we must not tell Isaac that God requires his death."

The angel started. She hadn't expected Abraham to agree. Not so handily, anyway. She fluttered her wings apprehensively and opened her mouth to speak. Abraham looked at her unerringly, his eyes full of the infinite weight of what he believed he had to do. She pressed her lips together. *It's his test, not mine.*

For a day they prepared. Isaac was excited about his first burnt offering. He was a lad of fifteen, clear-eyed and inexperienced.

As night fell, Sarah protested in whispers and begged Abraham to spare her son. Begged to be allowed on the journey to Moriah. Abraham adamantly refused, and as the sun rose the next day, father and son began their journey.

❖

WARSAW, 2016

The protesters gather in Lazienki Park, preparing to march on the center of Warsaw. There are a few men, many women, and one angel. She watches the hundreds turn into thousands, and worries. The beginning of a long journey is where the most dangerous mistakes happen, and she hates making the same error more than once.

"Things ought to be peaceful," the blue-eyed angel says, her feathers rustling in the breeze. "But did you bring a mask?"

Krystyna nods. She has a white medical mask with elastic straps to help her breathe if the *Law and Justice* party order the police to use tear gas, and a leather jacket to protect her skin if she is knocked down. Krystyna has never been pregnant, doesn't want to be, and finds the idea of having an abortion if she were a little terrifying. A government she did not vote for is about to tell her that she cannot do this thing that she does not want, however, and it makes her somehow even angrier.

"You can't really be a Catholic and march for abortion rights," the angel says; "if you go through with this you're going to have to give something up. Do you understand that, Krystyna?"

"I get it," Krystyna says, "I just wish you were coming with me."

"I'll walk with you a little," the angel replies, "to make sure you understand where you're going, and I'll check in again when it's over."

Krystyna gives an anxious laugh. The angel cocks an ear to the nervous chatter of voices in the park. It sounds like the insistent, pulsing murmur of an oncoming tide. She frets, and at the beginning of this journey, resolves not to hold her tongue.

"I once sent someone on a journey without being clear about why. Do you understand what I'm asking of you?" the angel asks.

"I know abortion is a sin, but I believe I have to follow my conscience. I know the answer isn't supposed to be easy. This is my test, and I have to do the hard parts for myself."

"And what is so important that you are willing to risk your faith for it?"

"This is my body. I deserve my rights. I don't care if it's dangerous. I can get hurt in this march or let that gang of old men chop away at what I am forever. Doing nothing is the same as agreeing, so I'd rather be here. I'd rather hurt now than be left behind."

The angel smiles, and suddenly draws Krystyna into a bear hug. The Polish girl hugs her back. She likes her guardian angel, even if talking to her probably means she's crazy. Krystyna squeezes as hard as she can and the angel's feathers are rough under her fingertips.

"You're going to do great," the angel says, releasing her. "Do you have your phone?"

"I have everything."

"Did you make a sign?"

"I did," Krystyna smiles, and unrolls it for her. It says, *We are the Granddaughters of the Witches You Couldn't Burn.*

"You're ready," the angel says with a laugh. "I always felt bad about the witches. Good luck."

A woman from the *Federation for Women and Family Planning* coughs into her megaphone, says a few words, and the women begin their journey.

Abraham and Isaac walked. Isaac made the journey look easy, but Abraham was old, and the journey seemed certain to take a full three days. They crested a rocky hill and gazed into an ancient valley with a river slithering like a glittering snake in its basin. On the far side was the low mountain at the heart of Moriah. The place of offerings.

Isaac helped his father up the last few steps and patted the donkey's rump. Something had been bothering him, in spite of all his excitement.

"Father, will we not need a lamb? We have our donkey and food and water, but what shall we sacrifice to God?"

"God will provide our offering," Abraham said, "whatever it will cost, God will provide the payment."

MANHATTAN, 2007

Banks always have the best air conditioning. Like they want you to come in just to get out of the heat, maybe buy a few credit default swaps while you're there. The walls are all very white, and they make DeSean want to paint. Want to feel the kinetic click of a Krylon spray can. Instead, he wills his hands into polite immobility while the bank lady explains the interest rates on his student loans. No one in his family has ever been to college.

"And so those would be the terms of your repayment, but remember that you have all that time at college to get yourself set up for when you graduate, and Chase Bank is always here to help you figure out how to pay it off."

"Cool," DeSean says, and smiles at the bank lady. She has a nice suit and wavy gray hair.

"Great," she says, "I'll just go print this up for your signature."

There are two chairs facing the Chase banker's desk in the little glass office. With the lady off printing up his contract, DeSean exhales his tension and looks over at the other one. The angel has been as quiet as she can be to let him concentrate on what he's about to do. They wait for a minute, but the bank lady is taking her time. The angel runs a hand through her short hair and stretches her wings. Another beat, and she breaks the mausoleum silence.

"I asked you to do what you thought was right. To pay the price no matter what it is. Are you sure this is it? You don't need a college art degree to be a muralist."

"Yeah, I do," DeSean says quietly, "I'm not good enough yet."

"You know how hard this is going to be to pay off? You're going to have to sacrifice a lot of happiness for this. Things you care about."

DeSean looks down at his hands. Dark skin, strong fingers, paint stains and calluses. The lady gets back with his forms before he can answer, but he's gotten used to speaking in double.

"This is what I want to do. I have to start somewhere."

"That's wonderful," the banker says, "just sign in the spots I've highlighted. And can I say that I think it's wonderful that someone like you is taking an interest in college?"

The angel winces, but DeSean just nods calmly and signs, like he's heard it a thousand times before. The banker rushes off again to file the paperwork.

"This is going to be rough," the angel says.

"I have to believe in something," DeSean says, "I have to find a way to say what I have to say."

He looks at his hands again. Artist's hands.

"And this is what I have faith in. I know what this is going to cost me, so I know I'll figure it out."

The angel reaches out a hand to squeeze one of his.

Isaac and Abraham made the altar together and laid wood for the pyre.

"Father?"

"Here I am, my son."

"The fire and the wood are here, but where is the lamb for a burnt offering?"

"Trust to God," Abraham said, and cuffed Isaac's head so hard the boy's ears rang. He threw his son on the altar and tied him down.

"No, Father, please!" Isaac cried. The boy struggled, but Abraham had performed the ritual many, many times before.

"God provides, son. It is not for us to second guess his caprice. He provides us this entire, fruitful world, and with his grace it belongs to us to use as we see fit."

"Father, don't light the fire, I beg you don't light the fire!"

"If God tells us to burn the world, son, then that is what we must do, no matter how much we love it."

Just as Abraham gripped the torch in one hand and his knife in the other, the angel returned in a frenetic blur of feathers.

PUYO, 2019

The courtroom is as quiet as courtrooms in Ecuador ever get, so not very, but enough to hear the final arguments. The angel shifts her wings self-consciously to avoid blocking anyone's view. The end of long journeys have their own hazards, no matter how well you prepare the ground.

On one side of the packed room sit the Ecuadorian government's lawyers. A squadron of impeccably dressed men with serious faces. On the other are the reason this trial is such a sensation. The Waorani people had come to court in their tribal dress, which is to say the same headbands and hand-woven cloth they wore in the rain forest. Each of them has a broad red stripe painted across their eyes. There is no metaphor to explain how incongruous they look; every other out of place thing will have to live up to their example. The angel doesn't attract any attention at all, even among those who might be inclined to look.

"This oil development is vital to the Ecuadorian economy. We must claim this territory, and we have a legal right to do so. We consulted with the Waorani extensively in 2012 and obtained their consent. If a few trees must be cut in the Amazon rain forest to ensure our country's prosperity, then so be it. These people will be compensated fairly."

The Waorani elders, two men and one woman, consult amongst

themselves. The angel leans in from the front row of seats.

"You have a choice here. That is the test. You really are free to choose for yourselves."

"We understand," the Waorani woman says, "but it's not so much of a choice as you think."

The angel arches her eyebrows, but leans back in her seat. *If they've decided, they've decided, and I have to let them go. Let them understand. Let me have asked the question clearly enough for them to answer.* She wrings her hands, but keeps pretty still, otherwise.

Nemonte Nenquimo, chosen to speak for his people, rises.

"The government's interest in oil is not more valuable than our rights, our forests, or our lives. They do not have our consent; they came to us for two days and explained nothing. They lied, they did not even speak our language, and we believe they have no right to take our land, destroy our culture or raze the earth. This forest is life, and it is not for sale. We will not stand by while you sacrifice it."

The Amazonians sit. Much later, the verdict will take six hours to read, but photos of the beaming faces of the Waorani will circle the earth long before it finishes. The judge will immediately suspend any possibility of selling the Waorani's land for oil exploration, and the world will rejoice at the victory of a tiny people over a state that failed to tell its people the truth. They will celebrate—not just yet, not until the ritual is over—but when it is, the whole world will watch the Waorani smile.

Abraham raised the knife high above his head. The blade reflected light from a burning red sunset. Isaac's eyes bulged with terror. The angel alighted in a wash of air that made the torch flicker.

"Stop!" she cried, and Abraham's arm paused at the top of its arc. Very slowly, he lowered his knife.

"I am still willing to do what you asked," Abraham said.

"No," the angel said, her voice trembling. "Don't. We're done here, okay? Just stop."

"I will kill at my God's command. I have faith as deep as-"

"No, my God. Stop." The angel struggled to undo the knots at the boy's wrists. She felt sick. *How can this have gone so wrong?*

Abraham, stunned, took a few moments before he put the torch down and started cutting his son free.

"We must satisfy our God," he said.

"Okay, fine" the angel replied, "just... sacrifice that ram or something." The angel pointed at a mountain goat that had gotten its horns stuck in a bramble bush. It bleated pathetically. Isaac, recovering from his shock and giddy at having survived his father's wrath, ran over to grab the ram. It bleated gratefully until Isaac started dragging it toward the altar. The angel exhaled with a whoosh and gave her feathers a shake. She glared at Abraham with her hands on her hips. It was hard to tell if she was angrier at him or herself.

"So God will spare my son?" the great patriarch sobbed. The angel's look became more pitying than angry.

"You're supposed to talk with your wife about what's right and what's wrong. You're supposed to understand what you sacrifice, and it's you who's supposed to spare your son."

"I only did what you commanded. What God commanded."

The angel tried to get a hold of herself and wondered if his ignorance was her fault, somehow.

"He's not going to choose who lives and who dies. You've got this backward. It's not about what God commands you; it's about what he asks of you. He doesn't need you to sacrifice anything to him, trust me. He needs you to make sacrifices of yourself. That is the test."

"So you stopped me," the old man stammered, "because I passed?"

"No," the angel replied, "I stopped you because you failed."

THE UNIVERSAL DONOR
BY
SAGE WOLKENFELD

Couldn't the hospital invest in eco-friendly bulbs or perhaps a dimmer? The brightness could make anyone go insane. Do they want to send more patients in to the psych ward?

Charles sank deeper into his seat as the nurse wheeled him around. They covered the entire floor at least twice by now, it seemed. How hard was it to find–the place that they were going? He gazed at his inner arms, which humorously resembled the back of a porcupine. His blurred eyes walked upwards along the tubes filling him with a concoction of fluids that were keeping him alive. A year ago, he may have gotten his lawyer on the line and claimed that the hospital had neglected to ask for his approval before inserting unknown chemicals into his internal organs. The lawyer would have defended Charles' freedom to be discharged immediately. Except, Charles had fired his lawyer two weeks ago. He hadn't needed the money-sucking vampire where he had been planning to go. Or, he would have, had he not awoken in a hospital.

The nurse finally pushed him into a square windowless room where two blank-faced nurses worked in silence. Captivity at its finest. His own nurse parked the wheelchair, exchanged words with the doctor who appeared in the doorway as she left.

The young doctor reminded Charles of his ex-teaching assistants. He was too polished, too green to actually know anything about medicine–the type of doctor who wanted to "help" Charles change his outlook on life. Every Jaden, Suki, and Brett in the university had begged for Charles' wisdom, which he frequently doled out outside his office hours. In return, he received lectures on morals, tolerance, and liberty. If the TAs had been interested in liberty, they would have let him dig his own grave.

It had been the perfect plan. The suffocating airbag that was supposed to lead to a better ending. The car that would become his world and burn with him. As soon as Charles was discharged, he'd rectify his failure and try again until it was done. Charles' eyes clamped onto his arm. Why wait until he was discharged when he could pull the plugs here? The initial concept of suffocation had been poetic: an expression of how he'd felt all his life. The daughter he'd lost custody to, the rank he'd been shut out for—all of it was worthless.

But now, the more he thought about how the bag pressed into his face, that moment of doubt flicked his heart, and suddenly he couldn't catch his breath.

Charles inhaled deeply, which proved to be a mistake. His clothes, particularly his sweater vest, still reeked of smoke. A nurse rushed over to him and changed a few dials on the machine. The other gave him a cup of water. When he stopped coughing, the flicker of doubt blinked again. He pushed away the cowardice. He was not weak.

The doctor approached Charles and introduced himself as Dr. Hani.

"Mr. Owen, I'm afraid that the amount of blood you lost is more than we have on stock. We've called in the universal donor to provide the rest."

Still slightly disoriented, he forgave the use of "the" instead of "a" universal blood donor. Twenty years of teaching College English gave him the right to correct the doctor.

"It'll be a waste." His mouth felt dry, his words cracked as they left his lips, but it seemed to go unnoticed by the doctor. A nurse brought him another cup of water while the other set up a second chair close to his own. Panic caused his throat to dry and he gave a harsh cough. In all his years of walking by the college's blood drives in the student center ballrooms, he'd never seen the donors give blood directly to the beneficiary. They used bags and refrigerators, not one of the long tubes that sat on the cart.

Charles could've protested, but then he would most definitely be sent to the psych ward. It was better to play along and waste their time and resources than to be relinquished of his freedom.

Dr. Hani gestured to a nurse. "Please bring in the donor."

A woman of no more than twenty-five entered. She wore some sort of scarf wrapped around her head and the only hair that peaked out was the half inch by her hairline. She was covered from collarbone to upper calf, despite the spring humidity. Sporty sandals covered her feet. Quite a few ladies attended his classes, but he'd never seen one who dressed like this one. Not Amish, she was—

Dangling from her neck was a chain with a circular metal charm inscribed in Hebrew. He'd seen that charm before—on the woman who snatched what should have been his English Department Chair from beneath him.

The young woman smiled at him. "Hi. I'm Naama."

"Doctor, I will not take blood from a Jewess."

Dr. Hani swallowed and pulled out a pen from his coat. "Mr. Owen, I ask that you put any negative feelings aside as she is the universal donor."

"Get another one. I will not take charity from people who take my taxes and are in collusion with the college boards."

"Sir, there is no one else."

"Type O blood is common enough."

Dr. Hani shook his head and sat in a chair beside Charles. "In this case, we refer to Naama as *the* universal donor because her blood can be used for anyone and at any amount. Every day, she comes in and gives our patients the blood they need. It's just as good as any other donated blood. Some claim it has healing properties, but that aspect hasn't been officially tested."

Charles turned his head to see if Naama was hiding a smile or laughing. Instead, she was sitting quietly in the chair beside him, reading from a small leather-bound book.

"That's impossible. People can only give blood every fifty-six days or so."

"Not the universal donor. In fact, if she doesn't give someone the blood, we lose the chance to use it because we can't save it from day to day."

"You're saying that if I don't use it, someone else will get it. And I'll get nothing."

"Unfortunately, yes. Your blood type, O negative, can only be replenished with O negative, which is why we are in this predicament." Dr. Hani tapped his pen on his clipboard. "Well, you do have a choice. We can give you the blood now or we can transfer you to another hospital who may have some O negative on stock."

"Fine. We'll do it now." Purging the tainted blood from his system would only be necessary if he had planned on staying around.

The nurses swabbed both their arms before hooking up a direct tube between them. Within seconds, the Jewess's blood entered his body. The nurses checked his vitals and then left the two alone. Every five minutes, one of the nurses would come back in to monitor the progress. Naama continued to read her book, nonplussed.

After the third check-in, she put her book down and closed her eyes. The cover had some Hebrew writing on it. Didn't she read anything in English? Charles found it ironic how he'd lost the chair to a Jew, which ruined any chance of making a name for himself, and now he was attached to one.

He glared at the tubing between them. This had to be a scam, the doctor's righteous idea to get Charles to recognize the meaning of life and all that religious nonsense. In his book, life was full of strife and then you die. And he chose to make that happen on his own terms.

Charles turned his head toward her. "What do they pay you?"

She opened her eyes and smiled. "Not a lot. Just enough for my time. I'd do it for free, but I need to pay my bills like everyone else."

Now he knew this was a trick. If she were the only universal donor, she would use her status to her monetary advantage. That's the type of thing her people–the economically incentivized– would do. They wouldn't volunteer and do this for free. When he'd given his time for free, he'd received nothing in return for his mentoring and coaching. Had he been given the English Chair, there would have been no recognition for all his time spent on ungrateful brats.

"Have you always been this way?"

She fiddled with her necklace. "I guess so. When I sixteen, I was stabbed in the back while walking home from school. It was dark out, so I couldn't see who mugged me." She shrugged like it was no big deal. "The thing is, I didn't lose as much blood as the doctors expected. They ran multiple tests, but thankfully, it didn't take them too long to figure out that my body replenishes its blood supply at a more rapid rate." She gave him a smile. "It was my idea to donate it; I mean, what use does it serve me to have an overabundance of blood?"

To make a lot of money. Charles rolled his eyes, but then considered something she'd said. Doctors had done trials and studied this woman extensively. Naama was young and pretty, despite her mode of dress. She should've graced many covers, bequeathed superhero status by society, and yet...

"Why haven't I ever heard of you?"

She fingered the cover of her book. "There's always a need for blood, and when my parents and I were first approached by the hospital about donating my blood, they agreed to keep my identity a secret. Those who have taken my blood are asked not to speak of this with others." She gestured to the door with her untethered arm. A wedding ring glinted under the white lights. "Dr. Hani will give you a confidentiality form to sign. I hope you will, because if there's anything I don't enjoy about donating blood, it's the endless paperwork." She smiled again and chuckled awkwardly.

Charles studied Naama, her slight exasperation creating depth to an otherwise doldrum girl and deleting part of the preconceived ideas he'd had of her. It was uncanny how she was constantly optimistic despite being brutally attacked on the street. "I hear that you're an English professor, so I guess we have something in common."

"How so?" If she said that she was related to the new English Chair, he was going to yank the tubes and leap from the balcony his nurse had wheeled him past earlier. "I'm a copy editor. The nice part is that I can work from home and take care of Aaron." She pulled out her phone, swiped her finger across it, and then faced the screen toward him. "This was taken yesterday."

He took the phone and squinted at the picture. Naama and a young man were kneeling beside a boy of about a year old. The boy wore blue glasses and dirt stained the knees of his jeans. The man wore a blue yarmulke, a lightweight camel-coloured sweater, and dark jeans, which surprised Charles. He didn't know Jews wore anything other than black and white.

He glanced at Naama and realized that she hadn't said one thing about her religious belief, how he should live his life. It was refreshing, to say the least, how he felt no judgement in this moment.

Charles' finger slipped as he tried to return the phone and the next picture appeared on the screen. The little boy was captured staring in wonder at a butterfly.

Charles smiled for the first time that day. The innocence spoke to him, filled a niche in his heart.

"Here." He held it out to her. Naama laughed when she saw the butterfly picture.

"Oh. That's too cute. Ilan must've taken it." She grinned and put her phone back in her purse. "He's always had an eye for detail. I'm definitely having that one framed."

Charles relaxed into his seat, pushing away the tug he'd felt while admiring the family. It made him wish he'd gone to see his daughter when she was that age. She was at least eight years old now. He'd always love her, but had he succeeded, she'd never learn all that he had learned over the years. She'd only know him as the father who couldn't deal with life.

"You have a lovely family."

"Thank you."

Charles stared at the blood flowing between them. "No, thank you for giving your time to help people."

"It's a blessing that goes both ways."

He stayed silent for the rest of the transfusion, his former preconceptions unwinding and reshaping. The nurses unhooked Naama first and she stood without seeming faint from the loss of blood.

"It was nice to meet you, Charles. I hope that you have an easy recovery." She slid her book into her purse.

He gave a quick nod. "Thank you."

She smiled. "Thank *you*."

As she swung the door open, he glimpsed Naama's son running toward her, and her husband holding out a bottle of water. He pictured his daughter flying into this room with five hundred questions on her mind. He'd make the effort to go see her since it was his choice to forgo the time with her. He wouldn't make that mistake again.

The young family left, grinning and talking while Charles lay in the bed as the blessed blood gave him back his strength.

THE FOREVER PROJECT
BY
MARK JOHNSON

"The attitude of faith is to let go, and become open to truth,
whatever that might be."
-Alan Watts

July 15, 2051

"Dad, I hate it here. I want to go home."

Daniel wrapped himself in his rain gear and sat close to the fire in a feeble attempt to warm himself. His father, John, sat next to him, also shivering.

"We're almost there, Danny. Just three more to go."

The night was black and silent aside from the constant patter of raindrops that had tormented them since they first started paddling. They had entered the wilderness by canoe four days earlier and hadn't seen another paddler for three, having portaged deep into the remote forest. It was a birding expedition. Daniel was three species short of photographing his goal.

"Dad, I don't care about the birds anymore. I never really cared about them that much. I'm cold, wet, and miserable, and you know what? I don't think this trip is really about birds anyway."

"What do you think it's about? We've seen a lot of birds."

"You know what I mean, not *all* about birding. I mean, we're up here for a different reason, *aren't we.*"

"Of course, Danny, plenty of reasons. These lakes are beautiful when the weather cooperates. It's a peaceful, magnificent place. When it clears up tomorrow you'll see what I mean. This rain is just bad luck is all."

"I mean, I think you have a *specific* reason you rescheduled your business trip, expedited your travel pass, and spent two nights arguing with mom about how important it was to take me up here."

"You think so, huh?"

"I do."

"And what is that?"

"I don't know, but I think it has something to do with The Book."

"The Book?"

"And I *didn't* read it, in case you were wondering."

"Was I?"

"*I know you know, Dad. The* Book. *The Book of the Order of Things.* I *didn't* read it."

"Well, how could you? It's against the law."

"Dale at school says Ricky read it before he...you know."

"Yeah yeah, went berserk, came to class naked, I heard about all that. How did he find it? You know they scrub the network for that text."

"Dark web stuff. There was a key going around school that opened it up for two days straight. They found like five versions, all slightly different."

"Danny, there's a reason that book is illegal."

"I know. *I know. Everybody knows.* Here's what happened. My buddy Jimmy Ratcliff read the first page and told me some things, and that's all."

"Like the setting."

"Right, so that's what I'm talking about. Last week at dinner I mentioned I know it begins here in the Boundary Waters. Next thing I know we're here birdwatching."

"That's right, Danny. *The Book of the Order of Things* begins right here. Right here among these trees and lakes."

"So I feel like you're trying to teach me a lesson or something, the same lesson I already know. I feel like this whole awful fiasco is about one stupid comment about me possibly reading one stupid banned book!"

"It occurred to me that we might have the opportunity to discuss it."

"Aaaagh! I knew it. I knew I should have kept my mouth shut. Look, Dad, I know I've done some stupid things before, but I'm not, like, a criminal. Everyone knows what happens to people who read that book. We all know about Greg Simmons who threw out a full ride scholarship to Oxford to join the Dearthmore campaign, of all things. And, everyone knows that once you start reading it, you can't stop, and that it changes you, or something, and that it is dangerous and illegal and everything. They *prepare* us for the possibility we're reading text slipped into unrelated manuscripts. Since elementary school they've drilled it into us–*father, son, wilderness trip, just stop reading, report the source immediately, or else.* You don't need to worry about me so much. I'm not stupid and I can take care of myself. I know there are slightly-modified fakes that cause permanent psychological damage. *I know how not to read it.*"

"Danny, I didn't take you up here because of that comment. And about *The Book*, I'm not worried. I want you to know you never need to fear the truth."

"I know, I know, they *always* say that at school...except for *The Book*. There is no truth in *The Book*. Only lies. This whole trip is for nothing. I'm tired. I'm cold. I'm going to bed."

"Okay, good night son. Up at sunrise tomorrow and rest that shutter finger. Our chatty rose-breasted grosbeak can't hide from us forever."

"Danny, wake up!"

"Ug, Dad, it's not even light out. It's too cold."

The temperature had dropped, and the cold rain continued to fall through thick fog as John and Daniel emerged from their tent. Chilled to the bone, they donned their rain gear and hiked through the woods, boots sinking deep into the mud. They found a clearing and sat in a bed of grass, peering through binoculars.

"Dad, you believe me about *The Book*, right?"

"I do."

"Look, I need to ask you something. And, it's something kind of serious."

"Of course."

"That first day, on the ledge, when I almost fell, well, that was a close call, Dad."

"Yeah."

"I tripped at first, but I caught myself and would have been fine. When you grabbed me, that's when I slipped off. You know that, right?"

"You think? Maybe. It happened so fast."

"I know you were worried about me, and I don't blame you. The thing is, after I started sliding down you caught me by one arm, my whole weight."

"Yeah, maybe I overreacted. It was a long way down. I guess my reflexes got the best of me. It won't happen again."

"Well, here's the thing. You pulled me back up. You pulled up my whole weight *with your left arm*."

"Did I?"

"Yes. Your bad left arm."

"Is that so?"

"You haven't lifted anything with that arm in years, ever since the accident."

"No, Danny, you must be mistaken."

Pleased-pleased-pleased to meecha!

John and Danny were interrupted by the distant singing of a chestnut-sided warbler. They sat in silence for a while, listening,

164

then stood and slowly advanced.

They forded a small stream and carefully cut through underbrush and up a shallow bank. The bird seemed unconcerned with their approach but was not visible through the fog. The singing stopped for several minutes.

"It was your *left arm*, Dad. I know it was."

"Hm."

"And it didn't even seem to bother you. You just asked if I was alright and we kept on walking. Since then, all trip, I've been watching. You've been paddling on your left side. I thought you wouldn't be able to paddle much on that side, but you have been, like half the time."

"Is that so?"

"Yes, Dad."

Pleased-pleased-pleased to meecha!

They heard the distinctive song again, this time more distant. The bird had moved ninety degrees to their right and landed about fifty yards further. They followed it down a rocky ledge. The stone was layered in shallow ledges making the pursuit quiet and brisk. They crept up on the singing and Danny scanned the branches through his high-powered telephoto lens, eager to take a shot, but the song had stopped.

"Dad. This is difficult to do, but I have to do it. Your arm. If it isn't broken, I mean, if you are able to use it, I need to report that, don't I?"

"Do you?"

"Dad, I think I do. If I don't report suspected fraud within a day I will lose points, my social rating will go way down, and I can't afford that. I mean, you aren't eligible for the disability credits if your arm works, and you know that. We spent all last semester at school learning about civic duty and accountability. I earned my Social Agent Status. If I fail to report an event and they find out later I lose my status, instantly. I could even be charged as an accomplice. I feel like this is a test–like I'm on trial. I didn't read *The Book*. *I didn't*. But, I *did* notice you used your left arm. I know how much we need that money, Dad. I understand why you would feel you need to do that. I know a lot of people do it, and I know that without disability credits it's hard to earn a living. But, I can't risk it. It's my future, my whole life ahead of me. I know we said no phones this trip, but I need to do this. I need to report you to Social Services. I need to do it *now*."

"I understand, Son. Do what you think is best."

Daniel retrieved his phone from his pocket and turned it on.

"Dad, something is wrong. It says I don't have a connection. What does that mean?"

"It means you are not connected to the network."

"Not connected? Wait. My Social Rating hasn't changed for three days. Something else is going on."

"Check your messages."

"Nothing. What is happening?"

"We are out of range."

"Out of range? What is this, the 2010s? No place is *out of range* anymore, Dad. You're *so* out of touch sometimes."

"Up here we are."

"What?"

"No place on earth is out of range, except *up here*. The signal is being interrupted. All the signals."

"And you *know* this?"

"Yeah."

"Wait. So, no communication? Nothing? What about GPS?"

"Nope, not for miles around."

"Well how do you even know where we are?

"I don't, exactly."

"So, we're lost?"

"I haven't known our precise location for three days. When they searched me at the entry point they confiscated my maps. They don't allow them up here anymore. I've been on these lakes enough that I thought I could remember, but at some point nothing was familiar. Since then I have been looking for landmarks and, well, hoping to run into someone. That big boulder by the shore back at out campsite I may have seen long ago. I think there's another site across the lake, but there's no way out other than the way we came in. Yup, we're pretty much on our own for now."

Daniel sat down on a log and put his hands on his face. He started sobbing. John scanned the area he last heard the warbler through the telephoto lens.

"Wait. You were searched? They took your *maps?* Like, *paper maps?* Dad! What's going on? How could you do this?"

"They're closing down the area to visitors in a couple weeks. I figured it's now or never."

"Closing down the Boundary Waters?"

"Yeah, only a few people know about it. They're going to set up a perimeter. There has been some illegal emigration to Canada. There are also reports of Anarchist hideouts."

"Anarchist hideouts? Outlaws? Why didn't you tell me any of this?"

"I wanted you to find your birds."

"What the hell are we going to do?"

"Keep our eyes open."

John handed Daniel the camera and encouraged him to take a look, then insisted.

Daniel glared at his father and reluctantly took the large telephoto lens and looked through the viewfinder. There it was, the chestnut-sided warbler. But beyond, through the haze and leaves, he identified the shape of a man. He seemed to be walking back and forth. Daniel started, astonished, then continued tracking the man who seemed to be engaged in some routine task, stacking something.

"Dad," he whispered hoarsely, "there's someone...there's someone up there."

"You were right, Danny."

"I was? Right about what?"

"This trip. It's not really about birds."

Daniel watched John crouch and pull a handgun from his rear

holster, then rack the slide.

"Holy shit, Dad. You have a gun? That violates..."

"Just be quiet, Danny. Follow me."

John and Daniel took a single stride into the forest when a booming voice stopped them cold.

"You won't be needing that."

John clutched Daniel, pulled him close, and pointed his pistol at the man who had emerged from the side of the foliage and was swaggering slowly toward them. He was a huge bald man in cowboy boots with a neat denim shirt and bolo tie beneath his tasseled leather coat. He paused, his palms were open to either side, and smiled at the duo warmly.

"You can put that away, partner. No one needs to get hurt," the man said.

"How do I know you're not one of them?"

"You don't."

His hands rose slightly, parting his coat enough to reveal large firearms holstered conspicuously at either side. Daniel looked at his father uneasily. John steadied his grip.

"But, if I were, you'd already be in handcuffs. Gentlemen, come inside and warm up. That's an invitation, not an order."

The man smiled with a nod and turned. His voice continued to resonate through the woods as he casually sauntered away.

"You don't have to come," he bellowed. "Hell, if it were my choice you wouldn't *have* to do anything! But, the fact is, you're here. I'm here. And we're all running out of choices."

John looked at Daniel with pain in his eyes as the man disappeared into the brush.

"Dad, I'm scared. This doesn't feel right. He says we don't have to follow him."

John shook his head with exasperation. "You really *didn't* read it, did you."

He holstered his pistol and began walking.

"Come on Danny, let's go."

❖

The large tasseled man led John and Daniel through towering stacks of firewood to a small, rustic cabin. They walked through the door and sat on simple log furniture as the man kindled a fire in an imposing stone fireplace that occupied most of one wall. His voice was no less imposing.

"When I got here, they asked me if I wanted to live forever."

John focused on taking off his boots. Daniel glanced at his father with continued apprehension as he untied his own laces. The man carefully adjusted the burning pieces of bark and tinder as he spoke.

"I said to 'em 'I intend to! So far so good!'" He looked back and smiled at the staring duo. "Yeah, they didn't laugh either. Heh, that was a pretty long time ago now."

When the fire was lit, he stood and discreetly reached for a flyswatter hanging on the wall.

"Point of that story being, well…"

Smack! He hit a log beam overhead with the swatter, then retrieved the carcass of a fly from the floor.

"…I didn't know what the hell I was getting into, pretty much exactly like the two of you. Yes, John, even *you*."

He pinched the wings of the fly between his finger and thumb and held it in front of Danny and John, turning it slowly to reveal the tiny fragments of micro circuitry. With a look of disgust, he tossed the bug into the fire, where it crackled and sparked. He nodded discretely to invite them toward the rear of the cabin, where he pulled a panel up from the floor, exposing a hidden staircase.

Daniel looked back at his father, who assured him it was alright. They followed the man down into a basement and locked a heavy soundproof door behind them.

The room contrasted with the rustic simplicity of the cabin. They had walked into what might have been the waiting area for a medical office. It was a plain, wide corridor with polished floors, rows of chairs, and office furniture, all dimly lit with a few floor lamps. Some paintings hung on the walls, warming the space from its otherwise austere atmosphere.

"The name's Jesse," he boomed, as he shook Danny's hand firmly, then John's. "How long has that thing been pestering you?"

"Since we put in at the entry point," replied John, to Danny's surprise.

"Ha! You still call those 'entry points.' Some summer fun and recreation! Those are official national security checkpoints now, brothers, they just haven't updated the signage. That bug was listening in, as I'm sure you know, but you may not know its bite can give you a horse's dose of neurotoxin, yessir, and all at the flick of the NSA intern's jittery remote guidance finger. My guess is the border agents probably sick one on every paddler, those bastards. So, anyways," addressing Daniel, "welcome to the Boundary Waters Canoe Area Wilderness. How has your trip been so far?"

"Um. Not all bad. We've been canoeing and portaging, and birdwatching, mostly."

"Ah, tweeters, very good. How's that going?"

"Well it's been cold and rainy, but yeah, we've seen birds. Two species remaining for our goal. We're almost there."

"Spectacular! Birding requires patience, hawk-like vigilance. You've got to keep your eyes open."

"Yes sir. Um, sir, I want you to know I looked for the scanner when we came in but didn't see one. I need to report that I didn't check my belongings. I'm supposed to tell you that, right? That I didn't scan my belongings for possible contraband?"

Jesse was listening but didn't answer. Daniel continued...

"This is a public building, right? Looks like it. TSA ordinance 13493 specifies security protocol for all public property. Sir, I just earned my Social Agent status and entry without submitting to a search is trespassing, and trespassing is grounds for revoc..."

"Danny," he laid a powerful hand on Daniel's shoulder. "This building has been liberated and is no longer state property. You have entered Rothbard Court at Otto Lakes. No search is required here *or allowed* for that matter."

"Also, sir," persisted Danny, "pertaining to the Social Security and Health Services Fraud Act of 2035, as a Social Agent, I am obligated to report any and all possible infractions immediately..."

"Danny, that's enough!" interjected John, his eyes piercing his son's like daggers. Daniel quavered, scarcely having heard such force in his father's voice.

John calmed himself and spoke deliberately, kneeling in front of his son.

"Danny, the punishment for reporting your father to U.S. Social Services is the one you need to worry about the most."

Daniel, surprised and perplexed, nodded reluctantly.

"You'll find more lookin' for birds, Danny," remarked Jesse, warmly. "Now! If you'll excuse us, I need a few words with your father. The game room is that way."

Through a small hallway Daniel saw the familiar seat configuration and controller apparatus of his favorite gaming system and excused himself enthusiastically.

Jesse closed the door to the game room. He poured a goblet of Orval and handed it to John, then poured one for himself. They sat across from each other.

"Jesse, I hate this. I want to come home," John groaned as he slumped forward in his chair, covering his face with his hand.

"Sorry, you can't. It's happening, John. The AI in the Konkin Cluster is learning faster than our models could have possibly predicted. It's a dinkum thinkum. We can't keep up with the data, the findings. We need more people. We need you now more than ever."

"I can't do it anymore. Every day it gets worse. You saw how he is. All the kids at school are like that. Automatons. And the ones who don't worship the system are hopeless and nihilistic. Little Jimmy Anderso..."

"We cycled the DNA and organic substrate through an increasingly diverse and stressful series of environment variable sets to trigger a prolonged epigenetic response. Through recursive winnowing with Bob's neural network we were able to identify several viable sets capable of stimulating the Damage Remediation Protocols we are exploring. We have escaped longevity velocity in several repeatable test cases. Our Saganaga team is evaluating a therapy implementation plan."

"Oh!" John continued, still following his own train of thought. "And now Julie in HR says I need to run an eight-minute mile in order to qualify for the new Wellness Platinum insurance rebate provision of the New Affordable Care Act. That's how they're keeping it affordable, damnit! Enforcing a health standard! I knew they would do this!"

"Pull yourself together, John! I get it. Mucking around up there with the Uruk-hai is tough. They're bullies, what do you expect? Stay focused and keep it in perspective. It's not all roses on our end either. Our Ogimunch lab is desperately short on techs."

"Ogimunch?"

"Ogishkemuncie Lake. It's one of our new submerged labs."

"Submerged labs?"

"Sorry to keep you in the dark. Progress has been swift, and we need to keep a lid on all this. We airlift them in. They come mostly assembled and we just drop 'em in the lake. *Plunk!* A team of welders fastens them to the bedrock. Ogimunch, sorry, *Friedrich Hayek Memorial Campus at Ogishkemuncie Lake* services a team of 25, located 50 feet underwater. The quarters are basic, but they have state-of-the-art equipment. Only 12 there now."

"You're dropping buildings in lakes?"

"Submersibles are cheaper than going subterranean, and more mobile. If we need to relocate to Ontario, or even the taiga, we can. I know how you feel about these lakes. Don't worry, the units are environmentally sound, fusion-powered, and completely self-contained."

"What about our budget? Aren't we still in debt? How are we able to afford this?"

"Nope, debt's gone. Jerry won the Mega Millions last year and paid it all off. He's our chef up there at Gunflint North. Mean spinach enchiladas. The proceeds will keep us fully funded for a decade. Everything has been ramped up as a result. Engineering got all new toys and production has been non-stop. We hardly have time to breathe up here. Just look at that warbler-borg that guided you in—completely autonomous and hasn't needed a charge for months."

"Alright, so, give it to me straight. Why am I here?"

"Performance evaluation."

Jesse stood and invited John across the room, where they sipped their beer and waited for a semicircular console emanating from the floor to complete its ascent. When it had, a map of the region appeared on its convex display itemizing the several dozen offices in the organization, along with statistics and status indicators.

"John, you're Recruitment, and we need to grow. The offices in red are starved of resources. It's not just development. There are mouths to feed and structures to maintain. We need farmers and welders, not to mention test subjects. How is it going out there?"

"It's scorched earth. I haven't furnished a report in over a year, much less a body. It's hopeless."

"Figured you'd say that. Maybe your strategy needs an update. What's your approach these days? How do you invite potential candidates to our venture?"

"Tell them the truth."

"A good policy. Go on...."

"I tell them life is hopeless suffering. I remind them they are frail, helpless, miserable creatures, and that soon they will be dead. I tell them they are powerless to improve their condition unless they accept responsibility for themselves. Out of the ashes of recognizing the irrevocable certainty of death, they have the option to delude themselves in unmitigated misery, or heroically accept the burden of their suffering willfully."

"And how did you get this job again?"

"Then I suggest they identify the things in their life that have meaning and act on those things, to act with purpose. I explain our mission, starting with the basic science. I explain that aging is not programmed into our DNA but is rather a consequence of damage to our body's ability to regenerate itself that we accumulate over the years, damage that eventually makes us sick. I explain that 'death by old age' is actually death by age-related illness, and that by repairing our body's ability to regenerate itself we can postpone the onset of age-related illness, perhaps indefinitely, and maybe reverse the damage that has accumulated. I ask them to consider abandoning society and joining the Forever Project to live a life of austere obscurity, underwater, researching regenerative medicine in hopes of progress in life extension science."

"Jesus. John, you're a train wreck."

"I know," John smirked cynically. "Then when they look at me like I belong in a padded room, I yell *'Alrighty then! Better get back to all that really important shit you have to do!'*"

Daniel approached the gaming apparatus. It was the fabled Z-Cube 2300, which had not yet been released. The familiar shiny red hoops and harnesses gave him goosebumps. He relished the chill on his flesh as he affixed the sensors, then strapped himself in. He was relieved the controls appeared to be the same as the ones he knew and donned the headgear. He leaned back…

"Dad?!"

"Hi Danny."

Daniel found himself standing on a rocky shore gripping the bow of a canoe. He gawked at the splendor of blue sky and popcorn clouds reflecting off the glassy water; the complementary spikes of evergreens at the distant shore. His father looked at him impatiently from the back of the canoe.

"Well. Are you going to pull me in, or what?"

Daniel snapped into form and reflexively lifted and pulled the bow carefully onto the granite landing. John submerged his paddle for balance, then stood and easily stepped onto the rock.

"Weren't expecting me, were you?"

"No, not exactly. What is this?"

"This is the loading area of the latest Z-Cube. You'll find this system is a bit more interactive than the previous version. It's tailored to your specific cognitive landscape, so your experience will be quite a bit more personal."

"It's too real, Dad. I don't believe this. It's really your voice. This can't be the Cube."

"Look." John pointed toward the water. The center of the lake bulged and a giant dome slowly ascended, water cascading off the sides. Ominous eyes peered at him, revealing the dome as a forehead. Daniel shirked in terror as the rock monster's hand surfaced near the shore, and as he stood, the full breadth of his enormous size seized Danny with dread. The face was somehow familiar, and he realized it was that of his childhood classmate Kevin. Rock monster Kevin chuckled as he used to when he impressed the other boys at Daniel's expense–when Kevin's desperation to fit in prompted him to expose the secrets shared in confidence, making a mockery of Daniel's deepest sentiments, desires, curiosities. His giant stone face smirked with an arrogant malevolence. Daniel felt, or rather *knew*, that rock monster Kevin knew everything–everything he had ever thought or dreamed. It was as if he had courageously disclosed the balance of his darkest secrets to Kevin, and in return Kevin was about to expose Daniel's life as a pathetic fraud to be mocked by everyone he had ever loved, cared about, or could even hope to know. It was all a hoax, a set up, and this, the Z-Cube 2300, was the trap door. And he couldn't get out. He tried. The game wouldn't let him. Though hardly begun, Daniel's pointless life had been a cruel joke for the amusement of, and exploitation by, fucking Kevin–rock monster

Kevin was the beast he had been running from his whole life.

"Dad. He's come for me. I'm going to die."

"Yes, Danny, you are, but not just yet."

Rock monster Kevin picked Danny up, hoisted him into the clouds, and chucked him with all his strength.

❖

John and Jesse shared a moment in tense silence, staring at the screen. Jesse started typing. A dashboard packed with metrics appeared–charts, graphs, statistics.

"This is a problem. Look at the data, John. The talent is out there. We seriously need to work on messaging."

"We need more than talent, and it's not *just* messaging. Our pool of viable candidates is limited by, well, other factors."

"What other factors?"

John sighed in frustration. "Alright, you want an evaluation? I'll give you one. You guys still piggyback off the real-time NSA surveillance data, right?"

"No, we have our own tools now. Way better."

"Alright, pull up my latest interview. It was in an old warehouse a couple weeks ago."

A quick search yielded audio, visual, thermal, and infrared.

"This one? Jack Diamond?"

"That's the one. Male, age 25, athlete, single, Hispanic. We'll only need audio."

"A professional baseball player?"

"In undergraduate he was a biology major. Discovered a pathway the Gunflint team is focusing on. Could be critical. He also happens to have exceptional strength and hand-eye coordination, which has afforded him a lucrative career in Major League Baseball. He has five batting titles and was elected league MVP last year. He still studies in the off season, just out of curiosity."

"Come on. What about art majors who dabble in bitcoin

mining? What about prostitutes and drug dealers? Retirees?"

"We've already picked the low-hanging fruit, man."

"Fine. Play it."

"Jack Diamond, do you know why you are here?"

"Um, yeah, because my chauffeur dropped me off at this old warehouse. You showed me the evidence you are going to send to my fiancé if I don't cooperate."

"Ahem. Sorry about that. Thank you for taking the time to speak with me."

"No problem."

"You studied biology in college, right?"

"I did."

"Did you then, and do you continue to, perform secret scientific experiments?"

"What the hell is this?"

"Because your work has been noticed by a private research organization that is currently exploring recent breakthroughs in aging science. Today, among our scientists, the discovery you made is called the De Grey pathway. We think it may have implications for the future of regenerative medicine, and possibly help usher in a new era of longevity for our species. We think we can achieve negligible senescence in humans, the elimination of biological aging. We think your abilities could contribute to this goal."

"You've been spying on me."

"We have. We have recognized your progress. We are impressed. This is a good thing."

"That's a violation of my privacy. Your second violation, by the way."

"We also know you are in possession of unlicensed laboratory equipment and illegal performance-enhancing drugs."

"Do I need a lawyer?"

"No. We're private, not law enforcement. I'm not here to threaten you. I am here to offer you a once-in-a-lifetime

opportunity."

"I'm not in the job market. I do just fine."

"What we offer is not a salary. We offer the opportunity to join a community of entrepreneurs entirely dedicated to the objective of eliminating age-related illness."

"So besides the satisfaction of my intellectual curiosity, what's in it for me?"

"You will be provided access to the therapy."

"So, eternal life?"

"No. You're still going to die. We will postpone death for a very long time."

"How long?"

"Right now, about a thousand years, but progress is being made at an astounding pace."

"What do you want from me?"

"Your intellect, talent, and companionship. The rooms are comfortable and private. We provide three meals a day, and snacks, as well as beverages and entertainment."

"Funny."

"Really. You will need to live and work on-site."

"That won't work for me. As you know, I have games all summer. On the off-season, I go to De la Fonte on Main each Tuesday for lobster. If I help you, it will be from the comfort of my hilltop estate and vineyard."

"I'm sorry, Mr. Diamond, but there are other, well, sensibilities we need to consider for this arrangement. For reasons that are no doubt obvious, we must operate outside the jurisdiction of any organized civil government. As such, you would not be able to play baseball and we would require you to relocate to one of our compounds. You are welcome to invest your personal property, once converted to cryptocurrency, either into the Forever Project portfolio, or into your choice of financial instruments available within the community."

"I'm not joining your criminal enterprise. Even if I were interested, disappearing from society looks mighty suspicious,

especially to my fan base."

"Oh, we'll stage your death. We do it all the time. We have connections with the best funeral services."

"So, let me get this straight. You want me to walk out of a Major League baseball contract, abandon my family, friends, and fans, fake my death, and move to some illegal, free-state dormitory with a bunch of outlaw geeks in lab coats?"

"That is precisely what I am asking. This is your only opportunity. You will not get a second chance. I know this is a difficult decision. At this point in my presentation, I typically allow the candidate a moment for reflection. I invite you to step back from your baseball career and remember that in a larger sense you are a miserable, pathetic creature teetering on the brink of death. The way to...

"Yeah, yeah, then you get all morose. I get it."

"No there's more. Fast-forward to the end. Listen to my closing."

"Here's the thing, Jack. This is the world you already live in. People are dropping out of this culture of coercion and incarceration. They are breaking out of this prison to pursue a better cause–devoting what time they have left to an objective more valuable than anything you will find on a baseball field. We came to you not only because of your science abilities, but also because of your character. Our surveillance tools have been gathering information about you for years. We know everything about you, good and bad. We know you are afraid of bears. We know you don't floss, ever. And, we know you wear a picture of your family inside your hat, every game. In a sense, you have already proven you have the fortitude necessary for longevity. You are not consumed by envy or anger. You are not resentful, or filled with hate, or possessed by ideology. For our part, the folks at the Forever Project have appreciated not only your work, but also your life. They are aware of our meeting today,

and they approve. None has voiced any reason to reject an invitation to our community, if you request it. This is meaningful, because, well, it is possible you will coexist with these geeks for a very long time. Simply step into the vehicle waiting outside. We will take care of the rest."

"Alright, that's enough. Not all bad, John, but trite and overall still pretty terrible. Let's go easy on the blackmail. It's not like we'd expect that here. Let's not insult their career either."

"Yeah yeah, well, in the end Jack refused because I couldn't show him evidence. When I offered to open up the science he got impatient, dismissed me as a fraud, and left. Being outrageously wealthy and famous did not help things either, of course."

"What if you demonstrated some technology? That could be compelling, right? Telekinesis? Perhaps you would have more credibility if you were floating three feet off the ground."

"I did that with Harry Beakerschmidt. Big mistake. Turns out he wanted in for the magic. I have to tell you, it's getting to me, all this. Every failure hits me hard. It's like I'm the executioner pulling the trap door. When they walk out it's like I am watching them croak."

"Don't blame yourself."

"Hard not to."

Daniel had never felt a gaming system simulate gravitational forces, which made the acceleration of rock monster Kevin's hand compelling evidence the experience was reality, as impossible as it seemed. Daniel squinted as the wind blasted his face, but he was so high he could only detect the green with puddles slowly passing by. The terrain changed to the characteristic shape of circular irrigated fields he had previously seen from a plane, and then he realized he was descending as he approached the outskirts of a city. It was his city, where he grew up. He saw his school. He was headed right for it. He was going to die as a missile crashing into his own school. He hoped it struck Kevin. All went black. He heard Kevin's voice.

"You think you're faster? Ha! Not even close. Hear that everyone? Danny thinks he's faster than me!"

Daniel looked around and found himself against the tile wall of his grade school gymnasium. His classmates were all lined up against the wall with plastic hockey sticks. He watched Mr. Moynahan, the gym teacher, step out to gather some additional gear for the impending floor hockey match. Kevin hit Daniel in the arm and prodded him in the side, taunting him.

"So you think you're faster, huh? Well why don't you prove it?"

Daniel knew who was faster, and the moment began to sink in. The simulation was so encompassing that awareness of the Cube faded, then disappeared, and Daniel became consumed by the situation. How many times had Kevin taunted him? And how many times had he gotten away with it? Many, many times, and a familiar fire was burning within him, a fire that had only grown since grade school, and he wanted to race, badly.

"Let's go. First one to the other wall."

Kevin nodded. "Ready, set, go!"

Daniel watched Kevin cheat with an early start and then snapped off the wall in pursuit, like a cat. The whole class watched Daniel approach Kevin, then pass him as they crossed the gym floor. As Daniel passed Kevin an eerie feeling overtook him. It was *too* familiar, complete déjà vu. Then, as he was about to brace the wall in victory, he realized he *had* been there. And, as he remembered, he also remembered what was about to happen, and felt his leg kicked out from under him. He careened toward the wall at speed, and all went black, again.

Daniel slowly opened his eyes to see his mother speaking with the school nurse. His head was pounding. His vision was blurry. Everything was the same as he had remembered; the taunting, the race, the hockey sticks. How could he have made the same mistake? Did it happen again, or was this the first time?

Everything was foggy.

The next day Kevin was serving lunch from behind the lunch counter where he was emptying a scoop of mashed potatoes onto each student's tray with sloppy carelessness. Each student thanked him as he did, as was expected of them. Danny held out his tray and Kevin smacked the scoop of potatoes down.

"Thank you," Daniel reluctantly grunted.

"*What* was that?"

"I said '*thank you,*' Kevin." It was the same, a grunting, defiant tone. As his memory of the event had crystalized, Daniel had recalled that day's lunch encounter with Kevin, always having wished he had the opportunity to repeat it. If he ever did, he would not cower in obedient shame and feign sincerity to adhere to school policy, and Kevin's amusement, as he had done the first time around. No, if he had to do it again, he would look into Kevin's eyes and express how he felt, regardless of the consequences. It was a tone he had fantasized about using for years, and even practiced. Now, having that second chance, he would speak his mind and let the cards settle where they may.

Kevin smirked and looked at the adjacent elderly woman who was scooping peas and carrots. "Mrs. Everly, did *that* sound sincere?"

Mrs. Everly could not say it did but wouldn't say that it didn't. She emptied the scoop onto Daniel's tray, hoping the line would move along. Kevin persisted.

"Mrs. Everly, I am requesting confirmation of a Courtesy Infraction, Code 1286. Can you confirm?"

Mrs. Everly closed her eyes, took a deep breath, then quietly responded "yes."

Later that day, Daniel sat in front of the principal's office, vengeful, with Kevin and Mrs. Everly on either side.

"Danny, this isn't like you. Your record is 100% compliant, and I don't know why you would jeopardize that? We say 'thank you' in appreciation of the service of our fellow classmates at the lunch counter. You know this. Kevin has reported a courtesy violation with Mrs. Everly's confirmation. Is this a fair accusation?'"

"But I *wasn't* thankful. Kevin was serving me against his will, as punishment, and did so rudely. How can I appreciate that?'"

"Danny, we need to show respect for our classmates.'

"I said 'thank you.'"

"Yes, but as you know the courtesy provision of the Human Rights Act requires *an inflection of earnestness*. The courts decided long ago that correct words can nonetheless incite or promote hatred, and we insist on dignity and respect."

"But I don't respect Kevin. How could I? Kevin has not taken the trouble to earn my respect or done anything worthy of it. He kicked my legs out from under me yesterday because he was about to lose a race. He gave me a concussion."

"It was an *accident*," claimed Kevin, smiling. "And besides…" The principal interrupted…

"You weren't supposed to be racing anyway, Danny. Look, I don't make the rules, but it's my job to make sure we all follow them. Maybe it will help if you understand the historical context. We are all subject to speech legislation and have been ever since it all started with Bill C-16 in Canada something like 30 years ago. At the time, disrespecting gender-diverse individuals by failing to address them by their preferred gender pronoun was, by law, considered an act of violence. At first, the Act only protected certain marginalized gender groups from discrimination. Over time, however, it became apparent that other less-marginalized groups were also deserving of equal treatment under the law. Why wouldn't they be? Why would a gender-diverse individual be deserving of respect under the law, and not others? These days, of course, the U.S. has adopted similar legislation and every recognized group is protected from hatred and harassment by the comprehensive language provisions of the Human Rights Act, including juveniles. Few have particularly enjoyed adapting to this in conversation, but it means you are protected from hate speech. No one is permitted to disrespect juveniles verbally without being subject to legal recourse, including other juveniles.

A simple 'thank you' is common courtesy anyway, isn't it? Danny, if you can't learn to accept the law, your life will be very difficult. I don't want that for you. I want you to have a happy, successful life, and in order to do that, you will need to comply. You will need to convince Mrs. Everly and myself that you can *thank Kevin earnestly* for the scoop of potatoes. Now, let's get this over with."

Daniel quietly burned with rage. "But I'm not thankful. You're asking me to lie."

"Danny. I'm not just asking you. It's the law."

The principal stood, as did Kevin, then Daniel. Kevin's smile was reserved but brimming with smug victory. Daniel took a deep breath. He faced Kevin, addressed him, then struck him in the jaw with a forceful upper cut, followed by a powerful left hook to the side of the face. Kevin stumbled back, shocked, then responded by lunging forward and tackling Daniel, knocking him over as well as lamps and chairs. The juveniles were eventually wrestled from each other by security officers.

That afternoon Daniel reclined on the cold steel bench of his cell, staring at the bare ceiling. He felt as if in a dream, wondering how he had arrived in such a condition. He had never broken the rules but had also never realized the knife's edge he had been walking between citizen and criminal. Being an outlaw was an unfamiliar feeling, but especially being one without shame or remorse. While behind bars, a part of him felt stronger, liberated. He had been incarcerated for honesty and had never felt more sure of himself. Yet, at the same time, there was an ethereal uncertainty subtly haunting him.

Pleased-pleased-pleased to meecha!

The bird call seemed significant and vaguely familiar. Perplexed, Daniel sat up and listened, unable to put his finger on it. In a few seconds he heard it again. He arose and gazed through the bars into the courtyard of the school's detention facility and saw the chestnut-sided warbler. Its peaceful, distinctive singing had a natural and numinous beauty that was peculiarly familiar, and as he listened it occurred to him. "The game! This was all in the game!"

The walls faded away, but the tree did not, and Daniel found himself surrounded by wooded wilderness again. He sighed with relief and laughed. The bird fluttered off but called again from the distance, and Daniel followed the call until he approached a rock outcropping overlooking a vast panorama of vibrant blue water and green forest for miles around.

"Have a good trip down memory lane?"

The resonant voice was Jesse's. He sauntered up the sloping granite face in his casual gate.

"It was, um, unexpected."

"What fun is the expected!? Danny, you didn't ask for it, but you have been born into a war, and you are on the losing side. Your teacher, your classmates, and almost everyone you have ever known denies your existence. They don't deny your physical body exists, but they deny it has its own mind, its own identity, its own dignity. To this world, you are a *juvenile*, and therefore endowed with personhood both socially and legally. You are a member of other groups too; race, height, economic class. But, according to the standards of your world, your existence, and any significance you might have, comes from your group identity. The divine sovereignty of your individuality, to the world you know, is a myth, and therefore so is your freedom of speech. All you are is an avatar of your group interests, and, as you know, you are conditioned for hostility to the speech of anyone outside of your interest group. According to this world view, members of different groups have nothing to say to one another, and in this context of human existence, where individual speech is rejected in favor of group power, we brace for inevitable violence. We brace for mass murder. I didn't say the unexpected is *always* fun.

"You attacked Kevin using the last available shred of meaningful expression available to you, the *real* you. You struck

Kevin because you were denied the opportunity to speak truthfully, to speak as yourself. The first time around–the time Kevin *really* smacked those potatoes down on your tray–you amended your tone. You complied and feigned gratitude in cowardice and shame. You feared the disciplinary consequences of doing otherwise, but you couldn't comprehend the cost to your true self, to your soul. Given a second chance, you chose differently.

"Danny, considering what I have seen, I am going to give you the opportunity to make another choice. This time, however, there will be no second chance. I invite you to walk through these bushes and forget everything you just experienced. You will return to your birdwatching trip with your father as if nothing has happened.

"Alternatively, if you desire to continue to confront the Kevins of the world and dedicate your life to the suffering it entails, I invite you to follow the signs. I can't tell you exactly what they will be. I cannot guarantee you will even be able to find them. I can only assure you that they exist, and that those who love you are doing everything they can to help you discover them. It is a choice that many have had before you. From this point forward, the choice is up to you."

Jesse began to walk away, then paused and turned back...

"Oh, and next time, Danny. *Run faster.*"

He winked and disappeared down the side of the rock.

Daniel looked at the bushes and clenched his fists. He peered into the woods and over the lake. He stared into the dense canopy above him. He waited, pacing, hoping to identify something, anything– a sign. The minutes passed into hours. His endurance and attention yielded nothing out of the ordinary.

The bushes were a sure thing, and he didn't stray far from them. They would take him home, back to the life he knew, and he suspected they would do so immediately. The boredom chewed at him, but he knew the bushes would also take him back to the person he was before he was thrown through the sky. On the other side of the bushes was a person less capable of confronting the rock monster–a person less able to identify its existence, a weaker person. He realized a part of him disliked that person, even though it was the person he was just hours before. His patience became exhausted, and as darkness fell he finally decided that no influence could possibly persuade him to choose the bushes. He would rather walk aimlessly into the black woods with nothing but a fool's hope of discovering some indeterminable sign. And that is what he did.

As John and Jesse toiled over the metrics on the dashboard, confounded, a man entered the room through a false door. He approached the two and whispered something to Jesse.

"Who is this?" asked John.

"Oh, this is Bob."

Bob and John shook hands.

"John, Bob has some news. Some good news. News that affects you, actually."

"Really? Okay, let's have it!"

"Ahem," coughed Bob. "Jesse, some discretion may be warranted in this matter."

"Bob, John has been here since the beginning. Hell, if he hadn't written *The Book of the Order of Things* none of us would even *be* here. It all started as his fantasy. None of us would have even considered it. He, *if anyone*, should hear this."

"You're the boss."

"John, Bob has just informed me that our developers have confirmed a non-invasive, robust regenerative therapy."

"Okay. What does that mean?"

"It means we've done it, John. We have the cure, the philosopher's stone. It means, well, we will all regenerate to our biological prime and then live forever, or get run over by a bus trying. It also means you're essentially out of a job. Having achieved our objective, we no longer have any need for recruitment services."

Bob took the controls and began explaining the technical specifics of the breakthrough to Jesse.

John tapped Jesse on the shoulder.

"Hey, psst, so, uh, what now?"

"What do you mean?"

"I mean, what do we do now?"

"We drink scotch, you moron!"

"No, after that. I mean, what happens to the rest of them?"

"The rest of who?"

"Everyone out there. Everyone else. Do we just let them, well, die?"

"You wrote *The Book*. Why are you asking me? The way I see it, it's nothing personal. Taxes, coercion, and death ain't my thing, but sayin' it shouldn't be theirs ain't either."

"Seems a bit unfair, doesn't it? I mean, they were born with that lot. They didn't ask for it any more than we did."

"Yeah, well, we did something about it, John. What's come over you? If you want to be a liberator, best find someone who wants to be liberated. If they can't even bother to look for us, do they really deserve a hit of life juice anyway? I don't think so! What's this about?"

"Ah, nothing." John turned his head, agitated. Jesse took a moment to ponder.

"Aaah, you bugger. Seems an appropriate time to recite a passage from the good book."

> *It's tough to bury your kid because they're stupid, so don't let that happen.*
> *The Book of the Order of Things*
> *Chapter 8, Verse 7*

"Jesse, I don't need it right now."

"Always liked that verse."

"And they're not verses. It wasn't meant to be scripture!"

Bob turned to John, matter-of-factly, and adjusted his glasses.

"Years ago, we launched a production team to account for this possibility, knowing a viable therapy would have profound implications for both us and for the remainder of intelligent, conscious biological life. As such we assimilated *The Book of the Order of Things* into an interactive Virtual Reality fantasy game that we hope will provide a means for receptive individuals to develop their powers of observation toward a mutually-beneficial interpretation of reality. This, of course, is the interpretation that recognizes individual sovereignty, disregards the authority of coercive institutions, and values life above everything else.

"Like *The Book*, the game includes clues that could lead a motivated individual to our facility. Of course, our enemies will have access to these clues. Fortunately, our enemies are not individuals, but rather the parasitic influence of anima possession that distracts them from the truth, and from meaning. We believe that an agent exposed to these secrets will come to abhor the false authority dictating his or her life. This individual will be stunned to discover themselves staring at the face of death. And we will offer life. This is how we liberate them. This is how we invite them to join us. In short, John, we expect that gamers exposed to this product will be better prepared to discover our efforts up here, recognize and accept the difficult realities of prolonged or indefinite existence."

"We are hopeful the game will accommodate this objective," Jesse summarized. "As a matter of fact, the production team has released a beta version that is undergoing..."

Danny burst through the game room door, then stood still, alert. His eyes were bright and purposeful. He grasped the camera in his hands.

"Dad, let's watch some birds!"

For more information about how to support the Agorist Writers Workshop and contributing authors, please visit:

www.agoristwritersworkshop.com

ABOUT THE CONTRIBUTORS

R. R. Rosalez lives with his lovely bride Nicky and their 5 children in the Southeast Virginia community of Hampton Roads. There, they are members of a local Reformed Baptist Church and seek to honor God through all they do. R. R. Rosalez considers himself a hobbyist writer who although he loves many works of fiction is also an aspiring history buff. His favorite genres are high fantasy, science fiction, and church history. R. R. is co-host of the podcast Church History Matters.
Twitter: @CHM_Podcast

Freya Wilde lives in and is from the Red River Valley of the North. Freya has published several times on ebook sites, and most recently has two books on Amazon, Oldfolk Fairy-tales, adult fiction and Eye of the Giant: Red River Adventures, juvenile fiction. She is currently working on a science fiction novel, and the second book in the Red River Adventure series, available at amazon.com.
Facebook: www.facebook.com/Freya-Wilde-1467004406657274

Roy Baird lives in Northern Ireland and is a retired firefighter. After retirement he has tried his hand at writing short stories, mostly for his own amusement. Being an admirer of the short stories written by Stephen King, it was to be expected that his would tend to follow the same theme. He has also written a number of serious articles which have been published in various magazines connected to his past employment.

Kaeding Sindelar writes agorist fantasy and horror. He uses fiction to illuminate the counter-economic ideas espoused by the great agorist philosophers such as SEK3 and *Oscar the Grouch*. His first novel based on his character *Malicyde Roth* will be published in 2020.

M. Allyson Szabo has worked as a telephone operator, a data clerk, a blog writer, an author, and as a mom. She began writing in her early teens, inspired by such authors as Piers Anthony and Robert A. Heinlein. Her family puts up with her, encourages her, and locks her in her office during November for #nanowrimo. She spends her weekdays writing, home schooling her kids, and running her home. On weekends, you can find her at Renaissance Faires throughout New England reenacting the 14th century.

Website: www.mallysonszabo.weebly.com

Amazon: www.amazon.com/Allyson-Szabo/e/B00IY0GMC8

Facebook: www.facebook.com/mallysonszabo/

YouTube: www.youtube.com/channel/UCdt4Sz7jkD2R8IR9PtWlG Wg

Shashi Kadapa, based in Pune, India, is the managing editor of ActiveMuse, a journal of literature. His short stories appeared in anthologies of Casagrande Press, Alien Dimensions #11, Spadina Literary Review, Escaped Ink, The Times of India, and Debonair, forthcoming in anthologies of Agorist Writers and others. Shashi is working on a book of short stories and a novel.

Website: www.activemuse.org

Facebook: www.facebook.com/shashi.kadapa

Twitter: @active_muse

Lela Markham is an Alaska-based multi-genre author who occasionally communes with dragons. Alaska is an adventure like none other, where the midnight sun of summer encourages extreme adventures and the dark cold winters allow plenty of time to write them down in creative ways.

Amazon: www.amazon.com/Lela-Markham/e/B00OQWYP68

Blog: www.aurorawatcherak.wordpress.com

Facebook: www.facebook.com/lela.markham.7

Twitter: @LelaMarkham

Joseph W. Knowles is a follower of Jesus Christ, a lawyer, and a lover of books. He lives with his wife and children in Virginia. After his first short story was published in *The Clarion Call, Volume 2: Echoes of Liberty*, he self-published his first short novel, *Defying Conventions*, in 2018.

Amazon: www.amazon.com/Joseph-W-Knowles/e/B07WGX9C2D

Blog: www.providencenotfate.wordpress.com

Twitter: @knowles_joseph

Billie Holladay Skelley received her bachelor's and master's degrees from the University of Wisconsin-Madison. Now retired from working as a cardiovascular and thoracic surgery clinical nurse specialist and nursing educator, she enjoys focusing on her writing. Billie has written several health-related articles for both professional and lay journals. Her writing, however, crosses several different genres and has appeared in various journals, magazines, and anthologies in print and online—ranging from the *American Journal of Nursing* to *Chicken Soup for the Soul*. An award-winning author, she also has written eight books for children and teens.

Website: www.bhskelley.com

N.B. Williams writes about fact, fantasy, and the realms between. A journalist and content writer by day, she moonlights as an author of twisted tales designed to make people question her mental health, which they do. Often. In between penning novels and churning out short stories, she wrangles bees in the Texas Hill Country and cares for a growing number of pets, all of whom consider her work too scary to read. She's currently working on a novel about Viking vampires and is toying with the idea of getting out of her pajamas one day soon. Maybe.

Website: www.nbwilliamsbooks.com

Blake Jessop is a Canadian author of sci-fi, fantasy and horror stories with a master's degree in creative writing from the University of Adelaide. You can read more of his politically-charged speculative fiction in issue two of *DreamForge Magazine,* or follow him on Twitter.

Amazon: www.amazon.com/author/blakejessop
Twitter @everydayjisei

Sage Wolkenfeld was inspired to start writing because of a dream one night in 2009 and has been hearing her characters' stories ever since. Sage lives in what she refers to as "The Tundra" with her husband.
Blog: www.sagethoughtsonbooks.blogspot.com
Facebook: www.facebook.com/Sage-Wolkenfeld-Author-219375665481049

Mark Johnson is an author of software documentation and non-state-sponsored fiction. His publishing company, Penelope Press, sells illustrated children's picture books at a fair price, and happily in trade for remuneration in goods or services. Mark has traded children's books for impromptu musical performances, light construction, and firearm training. In his spare time he brews hefeweizen. Mark lives with his wife, two boys, and very vocal cat in Bloomington, MN.
Website: www.penelopepress.com

If you enjoyed **Fire and Faith,** you can find more stories of liberty and voluntary action in **The Clarion Call, Vol 4: FairyTale Riot**, such as:

THE PIPER'S LAST SONG
BY
KETURAH LAMB

In a little German village encircled by hills, there lived a kindly Piper.

He played harmless ditties for all passersby, and all he asked for in return was a smile and maybe a few coins.

He played his shiny brass pipe, eyes laughing, lips floating, his feet dancing. So enchanting was he to all that heard him sing, saw him dance.

His clothes were pied; colors of red, of yellow, of blue. His hat also boasted the same, matching in its colorful way. On top of the hat of many colors poked a proud, stiff feather.

The Pied Piper sang his songs, danced his dances, and all around him the people nodded with pleasure.

As long as the Piper danced, all was well for the little German town.

His cheery melodies chased away any grudges, every displeasure, all anger.

The happiness in his songs united the people.

One day the King's army came over the hills. Through the valleys they galloped, into town to the people therein. Sent from the Pope, they brought ill will that spoke of danger. A danger that not even the Piper's music could withstand.

But the Piper played for them as he would anyone. He danced. He raised the pipe to his lips, capturing a tune, then sang this innocent rhyme, stopping every once in a while to let his pipe sing also.

I found a silver farthing,
a silver farthing,
a silver farthing.
I found a silver farthing,
A shiny silver farthing,
On this beautiful morning.

Now, you ask how I found,
how I found,
how I found.
Now, you ask how I found,
My shiny silver farthing,
On this beautiful morning.

My eyes saw a dirty mound,
a dirty mound,
a dirty mound.
My eyes saw a dirty mound,
Where lay a silver farthing,
On this beautiful morning.

The Piper drew the pipe to his lips and repeated the silly tune, then skipped in wide circles around the bemused soldiers. The small instrument sang rapturously.

The soldiers hollered, hoorayed, and hailed the Piper. "Sing us more, Pied Piper. Another song to ease our tired ears!"

The Piper smiled and continued to play.

The commoners of the little town were servants of the King of Germany, and of the Pope—who thought he was king of the whole world.

These people as one paid their taxes, said their prayers, and worshiped one God without freedom. Though the people had small arguments and feuds, they were like-minded—by threat of punishment and banishment. It was a hard time, but few realized this.

Except the Poor of Lombardy, followers of Peter Waldo.

They were different. They chose another life, another way. They wanted to follow God, not man, and follow their consciences and beliefs. They chose evident hardships over a safe pretense.

They begged the Pope to grant them this freedom, to let them study the Good Book for themselves.

But those in high places were angered by their words. Soon, these people were known as blasphemers, as traitors to God and country.

The Pope and the King wanted all to be one. All to serve the same king and the same God, to eat the same bread, and to drink the same wine, to be one everywhere.

The Waldensians refused. They practiced the true faith, hiding from the Pope. They lived simple, sincere lives, working hard in satisfaction and forsaking all frivolity.

The Piper thought them odd. He saw them as an uncanny people and wondered at their ways.

Could not all men follow God and Pope and King? Must one differ? Could not all live as happy and carefree as he? Who were these people that chose rags over riches, death over life?

The mere name of them made the Piper shudder with questions. Unanswerable questions. Questions he had no will to search out. For who would want to give up the joy of life for rebellion? They were not a pleasant subject to discuss.

And the King's men. All knew why they had come. To root out and exterminate every last one of these people.

Beware, Poor of Lombardy! Your time is drawing near. The end is now. The whole place seemed to say, in a warning, yet taunting sort of way. *The King's men, the Pope's army—they are here to serve justice.*

The Piper found his smile once more. Dark thoughts were not

for him. These people were of no concern of his. He put his pipe back to his lips. He would be joyful–play his music! This was life! He would live.

He skipped, jovially running through each street. His coat flashed brightly, and his pipe sang once again, glistening in the daylight. People laughed, cried, and cheered at his music.

They are the King's men–
Have you heard?

They wear their armor
In fashion and style.
They'll rob our larder
And treat us all vile.

They are here again–
Have you h-

The village gates opened. The soldiers, astride black stallions, marched out toward the caves in the hills. Their swords gleamed. The spears were sharpened. Armor and shield were polished.

All knew their mission. Death.

"Death to those who dare defy. Death to those heathens, those heretics, the Waldensians!" shouted soldier and common folk alike.

Away they sped, trot increasing to canter over bridge, vale and hill; through creek, wood, and field. On went the King's men on their horses.

The people stopped their work. The Piper's pipe was silent. No child went to school that day, no store sold goods, no fire was stoked, nor garden plowed. For off in the distance a massacre was in occurrence, and people were killed.

Though every man had just screamed for the Waldensians' death, each man felt something close to sympathy in his soul. These were neighbors, friends, relatives. Heretics, yes, but still...

Voices–screaming, wailing. All could be heard over the hills. The Piper put his hands to his ears. No music ever sounded like this!

The sun dropped low and shone red against the horizon. Its bloody light spilled over the hills into the town, symbolic of all the death below.

And then it was over. The sounds stopped. The soldiers returned slowly, laughing and talking of their wicked deeds with shameful pride, finding pleasure in their evil.

Amidst them walked the only survivors, nearly a hundred and fifty small children. A quiet anxious murmur of wailing rose from them as they were antagonized by the soldiers' cruel words and kicks.

One lame child lagged far behind and received most of the soldiers' brutality though he struggled to keep up.

Sobs and cries were stifled by a boot's quick kick or a spear's sharp point.

The people of the town dispersed, frightened and ashamed. Unsure of what was right, what was wrong, trying not to think traitorous thoughts against Pope and King.

"Served them right," they said to each other. "They had it coming." Yet, inside, all were horrified, and hid away from the children.

The Piper, too, hid behind a house, and watched the soldiers with eyes wide and scared. More forbidden questions arose. All his life he had been taught what was right or wrong. But how could this be good? Dare he even question this? Better to just ignore it. How could he bear what these people suffered?

How would he and his people live? For others, God, and truth? Or as cowards?

His heart longed to know, yet it wanted everything to go back as it had been yesterday. Peaceful, loving, joyful. Simple, without any dangerous questions or choices.

A soldier spotted the Piper and called out to him. "You, come here! Make haste, you coward!" He laughed at the Piper's walk–so slow, unsteady, and fearful.

"Play us a tune, Pied Piper. Hush these filthy rats. Give us joy after our long work!"

He withdrew his pipe and started a tune from his heart. Its sad beauty surprised even his artful fingers. The music seemed to say:

Little Children, stay your fears:
Rest and hear,
And do not cry, little dears,
Day is near.
All of the flowers still grow,
Sky is blue,
And all the creatures still show
God loves you.

The melody was soft, the tune comforting. The children dried their eyes. They remembered this promise and believed that life could be good again with all their might. Momentarily they had hope. And for a few short seconds, they were able to forget everything bad and evil, even the deaths of their families.

The soldiers, too, were touched by the beautiful tune, but in a moment, evilness returned to their words and eyes.

They prodded the children forward and called them horrid names.

They led the children down the street called Bungelosenstrasse. At the end was a church. The soldiers forced all the children inside. The lame child entered last, as fast as he could go, which was very slow indeed. Then the soldiers bolted the door from the outside.

"Ha, now sleep well! Just remember, it's your last night. At daylight the building will be burned to the ground as an example to all those considering joining false religions."

Laughing, the soldiers left the children to their misery. Off they went to drink and celebrate, leaving one man to guard the Waldensian children.

The Piper, too, lingered close, not able to leave the children. He wanted to sort through the forbidden questions, dangerously curious. He found a dark alley nearby and sat just to watch.

It was almost midnight and still the Piper could not sleep. The moon was high. The stars sprinkled across the night sky, and their light danced as if singing. Their voice grew louder, yet it was soft–like a child's.

Wait! It was indeed a child's voice, and no star. The Piper stood and searched for the voice. It was coming from the church, floating out, speaking sounds of fear and loneliness.

The day is dark, the day is gone,
Still I see your face.
And, even though I'm far from home,
I feel your good grace.

The Piper drew even closer. He listened to the sad voice, the beauty and depth giving him pleasure. What a sweet sound!

The enemy has found me out.
They have me in chains.
Oh, Father! Let me ne'er shout
Or surrender through pains.

Something glistened in the Piper's eyes. Tears of pity? Could this carefree Piper feel for others? His ditties and silliness seemed so vain just at that moment. So purposeless. They stood for nothing.

And though I never see the light,
I'll stay to what's true.
I'll remember to do what's right–
Hold me close to you!

The Piper looked into a window at the side of the church, the prison of the faceless singer; a death chamber for children. He soon saw the child, close by the wall. His eyes were looking to the sky through another window, praying silently. It was the lame child.

It was then that the Piper fully realized what he wanted, what he needed–that he even needed anything at all. He yearned for peace–true peace, like this child possessed.

Looking up to the same sky as the lame boy, he gave up his heart and soul. And on that night, he found peace....

Continued in
The Clarion Call, Vol. 4: FairyTale Riot